I0591214

Cast Them Dead

A BRIG ELLIS TALE

Also by Joe Kilgore

Insomniac: Short Stories for Long Nights

Fool's Errand

Cast Them Dead

A BRIG ELLIS TALE

JOE KILGORE

Encircle Publications
Farmington, Maine, U.S.A.

Cover design by Christopher Wait
Cover photographs © Getty Images

Published by:

Encircle Publications
PO Box 187
Farmington, ME 04938

http://encirclepub.com
info@encirclepub.com

To the Moviemakers

In Hollywood,
there's always a traffic jam
on the expressway to extinction.

PROLOGUE

BY MIDNIGHT, ALL HAD ARRIVED.
"Now that everyone's here there's no reason to prolong this. As we agreed, there are five pieces of paper that have been folded and put in this hat. They are numbered one to five. We'll each draw. Keep your paper folded. Then we'll all go our separate ways. Whoever draws the number one will return in half an hour and take the gun from the desk drawer. Once the act is done, dispose of the weapon as we discussed. There's no reason to ever gather as a group again. Four of us will never know who drew the number one and performed the task we all agreed was necessary. Remember, there was no plan, no meeting—in fact, none of us are even here. Right?"

Each head nodded.

By 12:05, all had gone.

~ ~ ~ ~ ~

The room was black as the bottom of a grave, save for the slit of light that shone beneath the door like a promise of redemption. Slumped in the overstuffed leather armchair, Abel Dane was in that dimension beneath consciousness. He had fallen into the deep sleep that whiskey induces before taking its revenge and waking its imbiber long before night has run its course. His head, and its accompanying golden mane, was tilted back vulnerably as it would never be in the company of others. But his only companion this evening was the bottle of bonded bourbon that stood half empty on the marble-topped end table beside him. The glass, which had formerly been raised to his lips innumerable times, was still cradled in his long, thin, comatose fingers. Their grip now nothing more than reeds wound round shiny crystal, warming an unfinished swallow or two.

The sound that intruded initially was not ignored, but rather incorporated into what passed for a dream in Abel's state of rapid eye movement. The short, dull thuds initially appeared as a judge's gavel wielded to call the court to order, then an empty tumbler banged on scarred mahogany to catch an inattentive barkeep's eye, then, as what they were, knocks on his hotel room door.

His eyes opened involuntarily. They began to focus slowly. Objects in the room transformed from shadowy lumps to furniture, paintings, a flat-screen television encased in the wall. *Odd how one can see in the dark if one's been in it long enough*, Abel thought. Again came the knock. He hadn't imagined or dreamed it. Someone was at his door. What was the hour, he wondered? Surely not morning. There wasn't enough light. How long had he been asleep? Impossible to tell. He wore no watch and there was no clock in the living room of his suite. Once again, the knock sounded. Neither frantic nor impatient. Simply repetitive, consistent, determined. *But why a knock on the door? Why not a phone call?* The lingering effect of the alcohol rendered him incapable of answers to his own questions.

As he made an effort to rise, Abel's heavy head lolled about on his shoulders. Pulling himself up, he noticed the glass still in his hand. He considered a quick swallow, but instead, casually released it into the center of an indentation his body had made in the chair. It tipped over and the remaining contents filled the leathery reservoir his weight had left behind.

Another knock, no more aggressive than that which preceded it, sounded before he could take his first step. Abel made no attempt to speak. He felt no compulsion to let the knocker know he was on his way. Keeping people waiting reinforced who was in charge, which Abel preferred. It taught patience, he often rationalized.

Hands rubbing his swollen eyes, Abel moved toward the door lethargically. Upon arrival, he peered through the tiny peephole and saw nothing but the opposite wall. He was about to turn and walk back to his chair, and his whiskey, when the knock came again, not discernibly different from the earlier ones.

Abel spoke without peering through the hole again. "Yes. Who is it? What do you want?"

No answer. Abel stepped forward and squinted into the minuscule circle again.

Still, no one. "Prick," he mumbled, turning away a second time. But before he could take a step, the rap sounded once more.

Now clearly agitated, Abel raised his voice.

"Do that again and you'll regret it."

Again came the knock.

Abel could have walked to the phone, called the desk clerk, and had security handle it. This was some kid playing an infantile game, he assumed. Or a hotel employee without the proper training, or the language skills, or the nerve to respond. Or maybe it was a member of his crew; too drunk, too stoned, or too frightened of his wrath to reply. Then again, maybe it was someone else. An ingenue perhaps. Too shy to answer but too smitten to stay away. In which case, any intrusion by hotel personnel would only be an unnecessary, and definitely unwanted interruption.

Knock. Knock.

"All right," Abel said. "I yield to your persistence."

He stepped forward, rested one hand on the doorframe, and turned the deadbolt lock with the other. Abel was reaching for the handle when the first shot tore through the door. Lead, fire, and wood shards blasted into his abdomen. A second shot quickly followed with a somewhat higher trajectory. This time the bullet and door fragments ripped into him just below the sternum. A third shot was higher still. It eviscerated his nipple and shattered the bone above his left breast.

The door remained closed and incredibly Abel remained on his feet. His shock was such that his mind was unable to keep pace with what had happened. He felt liquid running down his leg. His knees grew suddenly slack. They banged down hard on the carpeted floor. Abel instinctively raised a hand to press against the door and keep himself upright, or perhaps involuntarily, to keep the wolf at bay. He fell forward then, banging into and knocking over an occasional table and its bowl of potpourri. For a moment he was conscious of the scent of pomegranate, plum, and papaya. His ears were still ringing as he heard what he took to be footsteps walking away. However, the organ that housed his sense of irony had not been hit, as he managed to intone, "You might have at least waited for me to say, 'action'."

Then his eyes rolled back in his head. Abel Dane was stone dead.

CHAPTER 1

DEPENDING ON THE TIME OF day, the drive from San Diego to Los Angeles—the freeway drive—takes a little under two hours. Ellis chose late morning and the ocean road to avoid both the rigors of rush hour and the boredom of the broader highway. He preferred the winding stretch of asphalt that meandered through multiple beachside communities and exclusive enclaves for those with a lot of old or new money, often both.

In Newport Beach, he pulled his white 1966 230 Mercedes SL Convertible into the parking lot of a seaside café. Upon his arrival, it was not unusual for parking attendants, even the jaded ones, to flash a smile and deliver a quick and sincere line like, "Hey, she's a beauty. I'll keep her up front for you." Ellis was always pleased to see that some people still appreciated the classics and such treatment virtually guaranteed a larger tip than he might ordinarily leave.

Strolling into the restaurant, he cut an imposing figure with his suit coat thrown over his shoulder and his white starched shirt open at the neck. After leaving the service, he had been able to maintain a body that was still well-sculpted due to a daily regimen of running plus multiple isometric exercises. His six-foot-one-inch stature showed little if any signs of decline. Close-cropped hair and a clean-shaven face gave off a no-nonsense vibe. He was ex-military but not ex-badass. Ellis chose a table with a view and a Bloody Mary to precede his lunch. There was more than enough time to enjoy the food and the scenery and still get to his late afternoon appointment at the Hollywood Police Station.

His presence had been requested by Los Angeles police detective Ed Norman. While it was certainly unusual for anyone from the LAPD to be asking for help from a San Diego private investigator, it wasn't necessarily alien for Ed to be turning to Ellis. The two had previously served multiple tours in murderous hot spots that the military frequently left out of official reports. Ed was Ellis's commanding officer then and often chose him for assignments when loyalty was as important as lethality. Terrorists had to be taken out, often with extreme prejudice, but occasionally without written orders and almost always with maximum discretion. Ed never gave Ellis an order he wouldn't execute himself if their ranks had been reversed. Ellis knew that. He also knew Ed was like a bulldog when it came to accomplishing the mission. If an operation was scrubbed or aborted for whatever reason, Ed always found one way or another to get back to it. If any of Ed's men were wounded or killed during the course of a mission, Ed always found a way to assure payback. When Ed felt something really needed to be done, he couldn't bring himself to leave it undone. Ellis admired that about his former superior. So, while he'd yet to be given specifics about their upcoming meeting, he had a hunch that his old C. O.'s dogged persistence was one of the key reasons he was being summoned.

~ • ~

The utilitarianism of the Hollywood Police Station belied its fabled neighborhood. Reality seldom lives up to its image, and Tinsel Town's cop shop was no exception. *Just more innocuous brick and mortar*, Ellis thought, as he parked across the street and strode over. After checking in with the desk sergeant who made a quick confirming call, Ellis was directed to Ed's office.

Norman was on his feet with his hands in a file cabinet when Ellis appeared at the door. Even though a number of years had passed since their last encounter, he recognized his old squad leader by the broad shoulders and dark hair combed straight back. He was a little wider around the middle, but Ellis assumed prolonged desk time would probably do that to anyone.

"Got you doing secretarial work, do they?"

Norman recognized the voice and spoke before turning around. "Beats all-night stakeouts and cold donuts in the front seat of a car, my friend." Then he did a modified about-face and looked at Ellis, a man fifteen years younger and thirty pounds lighter than him. A man with what Norman considered a proper haircut, a friendly but lived-in face, and a body that still appeared to be mission-ready. Yes, this was the man he hoped would show up, and he wasn't disappointed. Jokingly, he added, "Plus a little filing now and then is preferable to spying on cheating wives, or running down lost potheads like most private dicks I know."

"Depends on the caliber of the cheating wife—or the quality of the pot." Ellis countered.

Then both men smiled and shook hands. Neither was a hugger.

"It's good to see you again, Brig. Really appreciate you coming."

"Hey, no problem. And thanks for letting me clear the decks

first. Got some open time now. Couldn't think of anyone I'd rather spend it with."

"I'm sure the fact you're also getting paid for that open time had absolutely nothing to do with it, right?"

"It was added incentive. But I think you know I would have come anyway. Still owe you for that tussle."

"Just another firefight as I recall."

"Yeah," Ellis replied. "They were doing the firing, I was doing the fighting, and my ass would have been nailed to their wall if you hadn't shown up."

"Score one for the cavalry."

"I scored it for you, Ed. Always will."

"Good. Then you can buy the coffee. Let's go down the street. The swill here would gag a goat."

Stir Crazy was the name of the coffee shop. It had multiple tables for two, a short counter, and one restroom with a half-moon on the door. Its glass front window was the daily recipient of the afternoon sun. So much so that the framed black and white photographs of various comic superheroes on the wood-paneled walls had faded to monochromatic grey. Three or four customers were scattered around the room with their heads down and eyes affixed to cell phones or laptops. All of them were young with various tattoos on their arms and necks, or metal piercings through their ears or noses. Ellis and Norman looked as out of place as Jehovah's Witnesses at a Goth rave. Norman's suit, tie, and white socks shouted "cop," and Ellis's suit without a tie made him look less official but no less authoritative.

After dispensing their coffees, the proprietor suggested they take a table near the back so their presence wouldn't discourage the usual clientele from coming in. The two friends smiled, understood, and chose seats in a far corner. When they sat, Ed's pant legs rode up a bit, as they frequently did when his belt was cinched just below his spare tire. Ellis couldn't help but notice the thirty-two caliber Beretta Tomcat affixed above Ed's ankle and just below his risen cuff.

"Uh, pardon me dear, but I do believe your slip's showing," Ellis quipped.

"Huh? What do you mean?"

"Your... uh... ankle bracelet. It's a bit obvious."

"Damn pants," Ed grunted. "Need to get these things let out."

"You always keep a spare?"

"Never know when you might need strength in reserve. Or maybe even a throw-down."

"That sort of thing department-approved these days?"

"No. But then most of the time, I'm not either."

"So," Brig said, "remind me—how long you been doing this now?"

"Almost nine years," Ed replied. "Traded in one uniform for another. Swapped putting terrorists down for putting perps away."

"What about your personal life? Couldn't help but notice that looks a lot like a wedding band."

Ed held his hand up and turned the ring on his finger. "It is. I was married. A widower now. Just haven't gotten used to taking it off, you know?"

Ellis winced a bit as he said, "Hey, I'm sorry man. I had no idea. Didn't mean to pry."

"No harm, no foul, Brig. Guess I wouldn't get those questions if I didn't keep it on. Been about a year and a half now. Her name was Louise. She was sort of the epitome of that phrase *my better half*. What about you? Ruggedly handsome. Tight gut. I assume hard dick. You must still be playing the field?"

"Let's just say I haven't found anyone I'm ready to settle down with."

"Well, when you do, you'll know it. But hell, if you can still burn the candle on both ends, I'd light that sucker up as often as possible."

"Only every chance I get," Brig responded, which occasioned a chuckle from each man. Then the conversation moved closer to the subject at hand.

"You like this outfit, Ed? They seem to like you. I mean if you're running a squad and everything, then you must be doing something right."

"Well, maybe. But I've got a cold case I can't get off my desk—they want it off my desk—that's why I'm turning to you."

"Would have guessed megalopolis outfits like yours had desk-jockeys who did nothing but looked at files all day."

"The department's huge, but crime in this city is nonstop. Our cold case crew is overloaded. I had to get the okay from upstairs to bring an outsider in, but I wasn't content to let it go simply due to lack of resources."

"Yep. Sounds like you, all right."

"Hey, things change but people don't. That's why I thought of you for this one."

"I'm all ears."

"You might have heard about it. Happened almost a year ago. This big shot movie director got himself blown away at a hotel."

"Yeah... I think I remember something about that. What was the guy's name?"

"Dane. Abel Dane. It was all over the news."

"That's right. I remember now. Never solved, huh?"

"Nope. Not enough to go on, or at least not enough to make anything stick. We had ballistics but no gun. Whoever drilled him shot right through the door. Had to be an amateur. A pro would have waited and made sure he was finished."

"What time did it happen?"

"Middle of the night. Around three a.m."

"Cameras didn't pick up anything?"

"Place shies away from cameras for the most part. Fewer prying eyes. That's why celebrities like it."

"So who knew he was there? Or who was there with him?"

"Didn't appear anyone had been in the room with him. But some of the people in the picture that had just finished were staying there overnight. Apparently they had this—what do you call it?—wrap party, and a few of them stayed over rather than drive home. The studio picked up the tab."

"Let me guess," Ellis queried. "They were all sound asleep in their beds when it happened."

"That's all we ever got out of them."

"Any with motive?"

"Hard to say. Everyone volunteered what a talented and brilliant fellow this Dane guy was. But nobody offered any personal insights. They all indicated they only had a working relationship with him. The investigating officers noted that each of them showed appropriate shock at what happened, but apparently none were what you call broken up over it."

"How many from the movie stayed at the hotel?"

"Five."

"Pretty small bunch for a film crew, isn't it?"

"The studio was willing to spring for some key folk, but not the whole crew. Lots were there earlier, but they all left on their own. Of course, someone could have come back, but we checked with the garage and parking attendants, and no one who left earlier, came back later."

"Someone could have come back on foot."

"For security, the entrance and exit doors are the key places where they do have cameras. No one who had been at the party came back."

Ellis put down his empty coffee cup and asked, "What about all the other guests at the hotel? Any early checkouts at weird hours?"

"No to your second question. As for your first, we interviewed as many as we could, but we couldn't completely lock the place down. Follow-up phone calls were made to the guests we didn't get to speak to directly. Nothing stood out or showed any connection to Dane."

"So you're convinced it's one of the five who stayed over."

"Yep."

"And other than the fact that your people are up to their eyeballs in cases, tell me exactly why I'm here."

"Because you were the best Intelligence Officer I ever had. And I'm betting you haven't changed that much. You're able to find things other people don't. You have a way with people, an ability to make them like you, talk to you, share stuff, you know? I saw you get all kinds of vital intel from one prisoner after another in the field... without threatening to gut 'em navel to neck."

"Well, like you, I'm not doing what I once did. But I haven't lost all my skills. What's the chain of command on this one?"

"You're looking at it."

"Got files, interview notes, all the paperwork?"

"Affirmative."

"Where will I be staying?"

"At the hotel where it happened."

"Is there a time limit?

"Think of it as a week or two vacation. Sort of a busman's holiday. We'll swing back to the office so you can pick up copies of the files I had made for you."

"I assume I can tell anyone I interview that I'm working with the police."

"You can."

"And it won't be considered a problem that I'm packing."

"License and permit in order?"

"Absolutely."

"No problem."

"Any restrictions on who I can talk to or how I go about it?"

"Nope. Just play nice—at least initially—don't forget to say thank you… and break as few things, or heads, as possible."

CHAPTER 2

Before the murder...

IRIS STANTON WAS CREEPING ALONG in rush hour traffic with a few hundred thousand of her fellow Angelinos. Every night she swore she was going to get up early the following morning and beat rush hour, but she never did. So she constantly found herself surrounded by a cacophony of irate horns, shouted expletives, and obscene hand gestures. *Why do I put myself through it*, she uttered to herself. It was a rhetorical question. She had answered it ad infinitum for the past two years. Two years in which she had not once made good on her quest to beat L.A.'s traffic tsunami, and two years to the very day, Iris reminded herself, that she had accepted the position of Personal Assistant to Abel Dane.

There was no need to pull over to get to her exit. She always got into the proper lane at least two miles before she had to. Iris was constantly annoyed with drivers who waited until the last minute, then clogged up everything trying to wedge their way into the lane they should have been in miles ago. She was like that. If people did things that really annoyed her, she made a habit of never doing those things herself. That way she felt not a tinge of recrimination for cursing them as the inconsiderate oafs they surely were. Under her breath, of course. Iris was exceptionally polite.

Once unencumbered by the snail's pace of the 405, Iris was free to maneuver her RAV 4 nimbly around the slower cars on Santa Monica Boulevard. She quite liked punching the pedal and zipping into any opening that presented itself. There was something almost Grand Prix–like about the way she darted from one lane to the next, never tailgating too closely or slicing it too thinly when cutting in front of someone. That would be inconsiderate. So Iris darted along the boulevard like some people scurry down a hallway. Faster than the amblers and the sleepwalkers, but never out of control.

At the studio gate, Iris flashed her pass, revealed a toothpaste commercial smile, said, "Morning, Frank," in a way that made him feel she was actually pleased to see him, and drove, as she always did, slowly past the long row of sound stages that fronted the street. Arriving at the office bungalows, she parked in the space labeled Ms. Stanton. It always buoyed her to see her name affixed to the stainless steel chain that served as both identifier of the vehicle and protector of the flowerbed. The swinging black triangle with the silver letters heralded her importance, her stature as a key cog in the wheels of this dynamic entertainment corporation. At least that's what Abel told her when he said the parking spot was in lieu of a raise.

Inside, she turned on the lights, the computers, and the coffee machine. It was a relatively modest office by studio standards. Her desk was just inside the front door. A tall rectangular window gave her a perfect view of her car and her nameplate. Abel had her name affixed to both sides so she could see it as she worked. For a narcissist, he was occasionally thoughtful of others when the mood struck.

Eight-foot high, sliding shoji screens trimmed in teak

separated each of five enclosures; Iris's office, Abel's office, a conference room, dining nook, and bathroom. Abel liked to open all the screens on occasion, giving the place the feel of one large, spacious bungalow. Only the bathroom had a proper door, and it was floor-to-ceiling rippled glass giving the appearance of a babbling brook. A Japanese fountain was just outside the door adding to the illusion. Another of Abel's understated exclamation points.

When she first went to work there, Iris thought the shoji screens would be problematic when it came to privacy. She quickly ascertained, however, that her boss had absolutely no concern whatsoever about others hearing what he had to say. And she came to believe that perhaps the screens' real function was to allow Abel to hear everything that anyone else had to say.

Iris checked the iCalendar on her MacBook Pro and printed the read-out for the day. She went into Abel's office and picked up the bulky file on his desk. It was tabbed *Things To Consider*, and it was filled with everything from script treatments, to storyboard frames, to headshots of actors and actresses, to pages Abel had torn from magazines. Any time he saw a photo or illustration that was particularly interesting, he would tear it out and put it in his file. It might spark an idea for how a room should look, or how a horizon should be filmed, or what sort of hairdo a particular character should have. A number of the magazines she had purchased for the waiting area in her office had several missing pages. Ownership didn't enter into the equation when Abel spotted something he considered to be visually engaging.

Back at her desk, she checked to see if there was anything from the previous day that she wanted to take with her. There wasn't, so she took one quick look in the mirror on the wall behind her desk. The face that stared back at her was ready for the day, she thought. Red hair pulled back into a French braid. Green eyes accented with just a touch of mascara and a pair of olive amber glasses. Starched white shirt open at the neck with the collar upturned. Dark brown leather vest over formfitting, sand-colored jeans highlighted by a silver belt buckle in the shape of a marauding alligator. She loved the way she looked today and the fact that Abel encouraged her to dress in any way that pleased her. Well, any way that also didn't *dis*please him. And as far as she knew, she had never done the latter. He certainly never voiced a negative opinion about the way she dressed. And he was not a man averse to expressing negative opinions.

The short, familiar toot of the horn announced the studio car outside her door. The car was there to pick Iris up before winding its way into the Hollywood hills to the home of Abel Dane. The director insisted on being driven back and forth to the studio each day even though his garage housed a brand new supercharged Range Rover, a classic Porsche 911 Roadster, and a congenially weathered Jaguar X16 Vanden Plas. Abel only drove them when the spirit moved him, which was usually at night and almost always when he was by himself. He preferred the image of the loner in the classic car. Sharing the spotlight was not something that came naturally to him.

The studio driver had an automatic device that would swing the huge Iron Gate open in front of the director's house. Then a winding drive led to the front of the 1930's Spanish Colonial two-story home with white-washed walls, leaded windows, and emerald green roof tiles. It had been renovated numerous times since the initial construction but each owner had maintained its classic old Hollywood look. The stateliness of the home with its muted sense of grandeur fit Abel Dane to a tee. He felt safe inside, as if the confines of the domicile tethered him to a nostalgic past—a past he put on hold each day as he made his way down the hallway and out the door to the waiting vehicle where he'd slip into his more public persona, the renaissance man, always above the fray.

The front door of the mansion opened and six foot three inch Abel Dane strode to the car with his leather man-bag slung over one shoulder and his signature Palomino hair bouncing about his shoulders. The forty-five-year-old had a prominent nose, deep-set blue eyes, brows as white as his locks, and a chin made for a dimple, but without one. He was dressed in what had virtually become his daily uniform; mock turtleneck, blazer, jeans, and ostrich skin boots. His was a look he had cultivated over time and was often described by the chattering class as defiantly casual yet not without style.

"Good day, Iris. You look particularly fetching this morning. Not engaged in any cultural appropriation with that outfit, are you?"

"Well, if I am, it's a culture I'm not aware of. Just a bit of Iris's bits and pieces you know."

"Oh, I know Iris's bits and pieces very well. Tragically I'm forced to gaze longingly upon them every day, but only from a distance. Always to know how they look, but never to know how they feel."

"That's a bit much, even for you, Abel. Long night, was it?"

"Just a bit of dialogue I was considering for the unrequited love interest in that period piece the studio's considering. Over the top, was it?"

"Way over."

"Don't bother to jot it down, then. What's the schedule look like this morning?"

"You have a story conference with Sam at ten, and a

casting call at eleven thirty. Nothing in the afternoon until three. Then you're supposed to go over the costumes with Zelda and the wardrobe people. If there's time after that, you agreed to give that Deadline reporter half an hour."

"Why the hell did I do that?"

"Well, as I recall, you said she had an ass like a racehorse."

"Oh, *that* reporter."

"That's the one. She'll check with me mid-afternoon. If you're free, we can have her come to your office."

"No, not the office. If the timing works out, have her meet me at the Formosa. I'm a better interview subject over drinks."

"That's debatable."

"Isn't everything these days."

At a stoplight a couple of blocks from the office, Abel looked past Iris and pointed out her window. "Hey, isn't that one of those new Bikini Barista outlets? Skimpy swimsuits and lattes, right?"

Iris turned to look. Scanning, she came up blank. "Where, I don't see anything out of the ordinary."

"Then you must not have seen this."

When Iris turned back around to face him, Abel had stuck his hand down his jeans and had his finger protruding from his fly. Iris jerked back involuntarily and looked at the driver up front. He had his eyes on the road and apparently hadn't seen anything. Or if he did, he wasn't about to let it be known.

"Jesus, Abel." Iris gasped. "What are you? A ten-year-old?"

"Does this look like a ten-year-old's?"

"No. It looks like an idiot's. Christ, we're almost at the studio gate. I don't believe you."

The director giggled like a schoolboy, pulled his hand out,

and re-buttoned his fly. "It was just a joke, darling. Losing our sense of humor, are we?"

"You're making me lose it. You know I don't like that. It's really getting old."

"Aren't we all," Abel replied half-heartedly.

Iris had put up with Abel's boorish behavior since going to work for him. At first, it had been simple sexual innuendo. He seemed to have no governor when it came to off-color jokes or snide remarks regarding her appearance or his. The concept of workplace harassment was as foreign to him as suits with ties. Eventually, the blue commentary had progressed to stupid stunts. Once he yelled for her to come into his office. When she did, she found the only thing protruding from his desk chair and staring her in the face was Abel's bare ass as he warbled the lyrics to Moon Over Miami. While this amused Abel to no end, it secretly horrified Iris. She did her best to hide her feelings and take on the aura of a detached sophisticate unimpressed with her boss's vulgar humor. But she was growing more and more concerned. She liked her job. She needed the money. It gave her financial independence, a small measure of personal prestige, and access to actual movers and shakers in the industry. But at what cost? Abel had never put his hands on her. He had never been physically abusive in any way. But a few weeks ago, an incident occurred that she couldn't get out of her mind.

Abel and a casting director had spent a good bit of the morning going over photographs of young actresses for a part in an upcoming film. He dismissed the casting director and asked Iris to come into his office. Spread out and virtually covering an occasional table were photos of beautiful women. Some were glossy headshots. Some were in various stages of undress. Some were nudes. When Iris entered, Abel was seated at the table.

"How can I possibly choose between all this beauty, Iris?"

"It's a tough job," Iris tried to joke, "but someone has to do it."

"Come over here and help me choose," he said.

As Iris was moving to Abel's side of the table, he added, "Which ones turn you on?"

Before she could respond with the word *none*, she realized the director had his pants undone and his hand inside his Calvin Kline underwear as he perused the photos.

Iris turned on her heel and headed away from his desk without speaking.

"Cat got your tongue, Iris? Pity, I could have used it."

Grabbing her purse, she bolted from her desk and left to go home. The next day, not a word was said about it. What was the point, Iris rationalized. Abel would just say he was kidding around. No harm intended. Couldn't she take a joke? There had been no one there to see what went on. There never seemed to be anyone around when Abel was doing things he shouldn't. Or if there was, they'd just look the other way and chalk it up to Abel being Abel. Iris realized it would always be simply her word against his. And who would believe a lowly assistant if a world-renowned director said she was just trying to exploit him for position, fifteen minutes of fame, money, or all three?

This particular day progressed without further mention of Abel's crude behavior in the car. His story conference with screenwriter Sam Brady involved a considerable amount of yelling, which was normal for the two of them. The casting call was for secondary roles that required little if no dialogue, but the look of each person was important. It was completed on time. The costume check with the wardrobe department was a catastrophe. Abel hated everything he saw and told them to go back and start over. But while Abel's day was going through its typical roller-coaster trajectory, Iris's day was definitely looking up. It started with the phone call.

"Hello, Iris. This is Cyndi in Mr. Brownstein's office."

Brownstein was the head of the studio, an exceptional executive who had guided the company to multiple years of record profits. He was also by reputation a dedicated family man, community leader, and all-around nice guy. Plus, he was the one individual on the lot that Abel wouldn't challenge.

"Hi, Cyndi. What's up?"

"Iris, I wanted you to be the first to know, I'm going to be leaving in a few weeks."

"Leaving? Oh, Cyndi, I hate to hear that. Unless it's something you want, of course."

"Well, it is and it isn't. My parents in Indiana are really having a tough time now with dad's Alzheimer's and all. I managed to find a position in Indianapolis that will help me help them."

"You're a good daughter, Cyndi. But I'm really going to miss you. And I know Mr. Brownstein will too."

"He definitely said he would, and I guess it's true because he's charged me with finding a replacement."

"That shows how confident he is in your judgment."

"Iris, you're the first person I thought of. You'd be perfect for this job. I looked up your personnel file and it would be a hefty increase in salary for you. Your administrative skills are excellent. You're attractive, intelligent, and articulate. And you must have the patience of Job if you can put up with that odious Abel Dane."

"Cyndi... well, I mean... Do you really think he'd consider me?"

"You'd have to interview with Mr. Brownstein, of course. But if I suggest you and Dane gives you an excellent recommendation, I'm sure it would work out. Do you think this is something you'd like to do, Iris?"

"Are you kidding? I'd jump at it. What do I need to do?"

"Well, Mr. Brownstein will probably want to speak to Dane before interviewing you. So you need to let your boss know that his boss will likely be contacting him."

There was a longer silence on the line than felt right. "Iris, you still there? Did you hear what I said?"

"Yes, Cyndi I heard you. I'll speak to Abel."

"Great."

"And Thanks so much, Cyndi. I really appreciate your confidence in me."

By four o'clock Abel had let Iris know that he would be available to meet with the Deadline reporter. She conveyed that information to the scribe along with Abel's direction to meet him at the Formosa Café in West Hollywood. Then she asked for a minute of his time to have the conversation she was dreading. He agreed but said he had to step into the men's room first. She went to her desk, reached into a drawer, put what she needed in a notebook, and took a seat in Abel's office. He came in and sat at his desk.

"So, what's on your mind, love? Need to caution me to keep my ego and my libido in check when I talk to this reporter?"

"No. This is not about that, Abel. It's about me."

"Ooh. How intriguing. Fire away."

"You know Cyndi, who works in Mr. Brownstein's office."

"Sure, I know Cyndi. A bit wide in the carriage and a rather humorless type if I recall."

"Well, you see, she's going to be leaving. And she… she wants to recommend me to take her place?"

"You? Take her place? Working for Brownstein?"

"Yes. Yes. And yes."

"Out of the question. You work for me."

"Yes, I know I do, Abel. But this is a real opportunity for me. It means a lot more money. And I'd be... sort of moving up in the company. You know?"

"Moving up? What the hell's that supposed to mean? How is it moving up by leaving a vibrant and talented creative mind for a pencil-pushing Jew?"

"Abel, that's a dreadful thing to say."

"Dreadful? I'll tell you what's dreadful. The thought of you wasting your time as some humdrum clerk rather than collaborating with me on important and prestigious films."

"We don't exactly collaborate, Abel. You simply tell me what to do and I do it."

"Far from it, love. I depend on you greatly. It may not seem that way. But it's true."

"Abel, you know as well as I do that there are many people who could fill my shoes. I could even help you find someone if you wanted me to."

"Well, what if I *don't* want you to? Is it just the money? Is that it? Is this your devious way of asking me for a raise?"

"No. It's the truth. I'm not asking you for a raise. Cyndi thinks I'm the best person for that job. That's why she wants me to replace her."

"Oh she does, does she? Well, what about Brownstein? What does the little kike think?"

"I'm not sure. Cyndi's going to recommend me, then Mr. Brownstein will probably check with you."

"Check with me. What do you mean, check with me?"

"Well... to see if you think I'd be right for the job. Or to ask how I've done working for you."

The pause could not have been more pregnant. Abel's eyes bore into her as a smile began to spread across his face.

"Yes. Yes, I guess he would want to know my opinion of you and your work. In fact, he's the kind of fellow who would be loathe to simply say he's taking you without my consent, isn't he? A fair-minded sort. He would want to make sure I'm okay with it."

Iris could feel herself beginning to perspire. It was all heading in the wrong direction. "Well, Abel, he is the head of the studio. I'm sure he makes his own decisions."

"Yes, and I just happen to be his current golden boy. The director whose movies actually make money as well as win awards. Do you really think he'd annoy me over the choice of a fucking secretary?"

"Personal assistant."

"Oh yes, personal assistant. That certainly makes a difference doesn't it?"

Iris could feel it all slipping away. "Abel, you know I've done a good job for you. You know I care about the work… and you. I've proved that time and time again."

"You've said it from time to time. I'm not sure you've proven anything. In fact, you frequently show a disdain for me that is unbecoming of one in your position."

"Abel, you know that's only when you behave so crudely and unprofessionally."

"Crude? Unprofessional? Is that what you think of me?"

"Abel I think you're one of the most brilliant and talented men I know. That's why I work for you even when you act so hideously. But I want to move on. I want to better myself. Isn't that what everyone wants?"

"What everyone wants is irrelevant, my dear. I didn't get where I am by considering what everyone wants. I got here by knowing what I want. Now, I'm hearing what you want. The question is, do you want it badly enough?"

"Abel, all I'm asking is that you understand, and that you give Mr. Brownstein a fair evaluation of my time with you when he asks for it."

Abel rose, slid his chair back with his legs, and walked slowly around to the front of his desk where he stood directly in front of Iris.

"I've never had anyone leave me before, Iris. Not my two ex-wives. I left them. Not the other studios I worked for. I was doing the walking while they begged me to stay. I find this situation exceptionally perplexing."

"It doesn't have to be, Abel. I'll find you an excellent replacement. All you have to do is be kind enough to give me a good recommendation when Mr. Brownstein asks."

"That's all I have to do, is it? Suck up to that boring Hebe?"

"It's not sucking up, Abel. It's just being honest."

"Okay, let's be honest. You know something about sucking, don't you, Iris. I mean you're an attractive and healthy young woman. Surely you've sucked a few in your time. Just how skilled are you at fellatio? Mr. Brownstein might want to know. And how can I be straight with him if I have no knowledge of your particular talents in that regard?"

Iris flinched. Her fists tightened on the arms of the chair. "Please, Abel. You don't want to do this."

"Oh, but I do, Iris," Abel said, as he began to slowly undo his belt. "You wanted honesty. Well, I'll be honest. You just slip those lovely lips of yours around what I'm about to pull out… just this one time… and you can get what you want. I'll give you an exceedingly grand recommendation to the pork-averse Mr. Brownstein."

Even as she continued to sit, Iris's knees were shaking, but she managed to steady herself. Keeping her eyes on Abel's face, rather than that which was about to be put in front of her own, Iris slowly opened the notebook in her lap revealing the miniature audio recorder she had brought with her into the room.

"This is all I need to get what I want, Abel. I hoped I wouldn't have to use it. I still don't have to… if you do what's right."

Abel didn't hesitate. He lunged forward and grabbed Iris's hand. Then he twisted it violently until the recorder fell to the floor. Before she could recover, Abel stomped one, two, then a third time on the device with his cowboy boot before it shattered.

Still seated, stunned, and rubbing her bruised wrist, Iris tried as best she could to keep the tears from forming in her eyes, but she was unsuccessful.

Abel quickly refastened his belt, picked up the smashed recorder, and dropped it in his coat pocket. As he was walking out, he said, "Going to The Formosa to see that reporter. We'll talk about this tomorrow."

Iris knew they wouldn't. She also knew that unless she gave in to Abel's abhorrent advances, there wasn't a chance in hell that he would say positive things about her to Brownstein. In fact, she harbored little hope that he'd do so even if she acquiesced. The bastard!

CHAPTER 3

AFTER RETURNING TO NORMAN'S OFFICE and picking up the files, Ellis got back into his car, wound his way to Sunset Boulevard, then up the hill to the Chateau Marmont. Norman told him that The LAPD had arranged accommodations for the P. I. at a drastically discounted rate in hopes that being at the murder site would hasten his investigation. Leaving his car with the fabled hotel's longtime garage attendants, he strode across the polished Saltio tile lobby and checked in. Once shown to his room, Ellis settled in for a quiet evening of room service and file reading.

As Norman had told him, other than the victim, Abel Dane, five people connected to the recently finished film, and the ensuing wrap party, had stayed at the hotel the night of the murder. Ellis checked the list. There was the director's personal assistant, Iris Stanton, the screenwriter, Sam Brady, the cinematographer, Yuri Kaminski, and two of the film's actors, Jocelyn Hayward, the female lead, and Zach Richards, the star of the picture. According to the notes, a man named Terrance Wayland was the producer of the film and the individual who picked up the sizable check for the festivities. He lived relatively close by, however, so he chose to spend the night in his own bed.

Reading through reports of the initial interviews with each of the individuals, nothing seemed out of the ordinary. Each claimed to have been sound asleep throughout the night, and none supposedly learned of the director's death until they were awakened by the police and informed of the murder. None of the five were staying on the same floor as the victim, so it wasn't surprising that none claimed to have heard gunshots. The file pointed out that even the guests who were on the same floor as the deceased claimed to hear nothing, leaving the investigating officers to note the potential use of a silencer. Clearly, there were good reasons this case had yet to be solved. There was little, if any, physical evidence to go on, and so far, of the five primary suspects, no one had more of a motive than anyone else. How much digging into relationships had been done? Ellis didn't know for sure. But probably not enough, or his old commanding officer wouldn't have called him. The next day he'd begin some one-on-one time. However, he still had one more thing he wanted to do that night. So Ellis set the pulse alarm on his watch for three a.m.

He was still half-dressed when the buzzing on his wrist awakened him. After splashing his face with a handful of water from the bathroom sink, he slipped on his shirt and left his room. Ellis first went to the lobby, simply to get a feel for what the traffic, or lack of it, was at that time. There were a couple of what Ellis assumed were guests. The two men looked a bit worse for wear as they sat in tufted armchairs and engaged in a conversation that Ellis surmised had been going on for some time. Other than a female clerk behind the desk, there was no one else in the lobby.

Ellis got back in the elevator and took it to the fourth floor where the murder had occurred. He stepped into the hallway and found it vacant. Walking to the room that Dane had occupied, Ellis stood before the door and tried to imagine the events of that night. He made note of the fact that there was enough room on either side of the door for the assailant to move and be hidden from anyone gazing through the peephole. He stood directly in front of the door, raised his right arm, moved his fingers into the shape of a gun, and tried to gauge where the bullets would have entered. Then he reminded himself to take a second look at the crime scene photos of the damaged door. At just over six feet, Ellis could imagine where he would aim, but how tall was the killer? And what did the file say about the height of the director? Were there any references to the trajectory of the slugs? Up? Down? Straight? Had the thickness of the door altered the angle when the bullets tore through? He couldn't remember. He'd have to go back over what he'd already read. But as he stood there taking the place of the phantom murderer, he had a premonition that the answers he was seeking wouldn't be found in the details that had already been assembled. Solving this case was going to require some face-to-face time with the five suspects. One of which stood here that night and pumped three slugs into a man on the other side of the door. An amateur, Norman had suggested. Probably true, Ellis thought. But it was an amateur that got the job done.

At nine o'clock the following morning, a phone rang in the outer office of Wesley Brownstein. It wasn't the phone on the desk. It was his Personal Assistant's cell. She didn't recognize the number, but she answered anyway.

"Hello."

"Ms. Stanton? Iris Stanton?"

"Yes."

"I'm based in San Diego, but I'm helping out at the request of a friend of mine in the LAPD. They're a bit overloaded at the moment, so he asked if I could lend a hand with the Abel Dane cold case."

"Well, it's been almost a year now, hasn't it? I mean, how long do they keep those kinds of investigations going?"

"Depends," Ellis replied. "Sort of a case-by-case thing. You know there's no statute of limitations on murder. As far as this one goes, the detective overseeing the case is a bit of a fanatic. Doesn't like to see any case go unsolved."

"I see, but like I said, I talked with the officers extensively at the time of the... tragedy."

The waitress stopped at their table. "So, what are you two having?"

Iris spoke quickly. "As it turns out, I don't really have the time I thought I had. I'm not going to order anything. Why don't you go ahead and order, Mr. Ellis? We can talk while it's being prepared. Then I'm afraid I'll have to get back to the office."

"Sure," Brig replied as the waitress cocked her hip and raised her pencil. "Got anything resembling a chicken salad sandwich?"

"We do."

"Fine. Give me that and a Pellegrino like Ms. Stanton is having."

"Whoa. Big spenders, huh? You got it." Then she walked away.

"It does get crowded here at lunch. I'm sorry. When we talked on the phone, I didn't realize I'd have to get back to the office so soon. Something's come up."

"Completely understand. Let's jump right in then. You were Mr. Dane's personal assistant. So, what have you been doing since then?"

"I'm now doing a similar job for Mr. Brownstein. He's the head of the studio."

"Sounds like a promotion. Working directly for the head man."

"Yes, you could say it was a move up."

"Did Mr. Dane help you get that job?"

"Uh, no. I was still working for him at the time. You know, when he was killed."

"Oh, that's right, I forgot." Ellis lied. "What kind of guy was Dane? Easy to work with, or hard?"

"He was a very mercurial type. A lot of creative people are. It was very challenging keeping up with him. But it was exciting too."

"How about personally? Did he treat you well? And other people he worked with?"

"He could be very demanding. But as I told the police at the time, we had a typical working relationship. As for other people, it depended on who they were and what they did, or didn't do. He could be very caustic with people he thought weren't putting as much into his projects as they should."

"And who might some of those people be?"

"Well, it seemed that he and Sam Brady were often yelling at each other. But I got the feeling that was simply the way they worked. A lot of squabbling, then a lot of making up."

"Mr. Brady is a screenwriter who worked with Dane a lot, right?"

"That's right."

"Any others?"

"Mr. Ellis, you have to remember that Mr. Dane worked with countless people on films. It would be impossible for me to recall everyone he had the occasional run-in with."

"I understand that, Ms. Stanton, but in your role daily... well you were probably the closest person to him professionally. So you might know more about individuals he didn't get along with."

"I really can't say, Mr. Ellis. Unless something happened in the office or on a film set, I just wouldn't know that much about it. He was very private about his personal life. He didn't share things that were unrelated to whatever movie he was working on."

"Well, if anything does pop back into your head about any confrontations Mr. Dane might have had, I would certainly appreciate you getting back in touch with me and letting me know. Even seemingly minor things can be important."

"I'll do that."

"Here's your chicken salad and Pellegrino," the waitress snarked. "Go crazy."

"I am sorry, but I do have to get back to the office now, Mr. Ellis."

"There is one other thing you could help me with Ms. Stanton."

"What's that?"

"Could you arrange for me to get on the studio lot and visit the office where Mr. Dane worked? The police could set that up but I'm sure it could be done a lot more quickly if you simply checked with the appropriate people."

"But why do you want to see where he worked? The... I mean... well, where it happened was at the hotel."

"Yes, I know, but seeing his daily environment might give me some worthwhile insights. I won't bother anyone; I just want to look around a bit."

"All right, I'll make the calls and set things up. When would you like to do this?"

"Later this afternoon would be good."

"So soon?"

Ellis simply nodded his head.

"Well, let's say four o'clock then. I'll alert the right people. Just give the guard at the studio entrance your name, he'll direct you to Mr. Dane's former office. Though, I'm not sure if it is as it was before I took my new position. I haven't been back to that part of the studio."

"No problem. I'll ask around. And I appreciate your help, Ms. Stanton. Hope you won't mind if I need to call you again should something come up. And, you have my number if anything does come to mind."

"Yes. I have it. Sorry again that I have to run. Enjoy your lunch."

Ellis was going to say, "Looking forward to it." But she had turned and walked away before he could finish his sentence, much less his sandwich.

CHAPTER 4

A T FOUR O'CLOCK, ELLIS ROLLED up to the studio gate. As she said she would, Iris had contacted the guard. He checked Ellis's name off the list and provided directions to Abel Dane's former office suite. Ellis parked in front and entered through the unlocked door. There was a young man in the outer office seated at a desk behind a laptop computer. The remainder of the suite looked empty.

"Hello, my name is Brig Ellis. This used to be Abel Dane's office suite, right?"

"Yeah," the young man replied, not bothering to rise or offer a handshake. "We got a call from Mr. Brownstein's office saying you would be coming over this afternoon."

"Are you the only one here?"

"Yep. But I don't work here. I'm just here to unlock and let you look around. Are you thinking about renting the place?"

"No," Ellis answered, realizing the kid was simply some kind of underling and had not been told why the P. I. was coming over. But if he was on the studio payroll, then he might know a little. "Do you know if this office suite has been occupied since Mr. Dane's death?"

"Yeah, there was an independent company that sublet it while they were finishing a picture the studio bought. They were here for a few months. But I don't think there's been anyone else since then."

"When did they move out?"

"Oh, I guess about a month ago. Something like that."

"How about the furnishings? Were they all here when that company took over or did they refurnish?"

"I'm pretty sure all this stuff was here before. They took the space as it was."

"Okay, thanks. I'll just look around a bit," Ellis said, feeling no compunction to fill the young man in on why he was there since, apparently, no one else had felt the need either.

"Sure. Go ahead. I'll lock up when you leave."

Ellis strolled leisurely about the space. The shoji screens were all in place, giving the area a more compartmentalized feel. He drifted into the conference room and didn't see anything that looked unusual. A table that could comfortably sit eight or ten was in the middle of the space with chairs surrounding it. A large credenza was at one end. Ellis wandered over and looked inside the drawers. They were all empty. He then went to what he assumed was Abel Dane's office, and that's where normality ended.

Inside the space was a desk unlike any he had ever seen before. Surely, he thought, this is one of a kind. It was totally wooden—drawers, supports, knobs, and screws, all made of wood. Even apparently, the air valves. Yes, this was a first for Ellis, a pipe organ desk. The working desktop was constructed of three six-by-six slabs that provided ample space for office equipment, papers, and whatever else might be required. There were six small drawers of varying sizes stacked horizontally across the top of the desk, and three larger same-size drawers on either side. Unable to keep his curiosity at bay, Ellis opened one of the small drawers to see if anything had been left inside. When he pulled the drawer out, air was directed into the organ pipes and a note sounded. He pushed the empty drawer in quickly and another sound was emitted.

"You've got to be kidding," Ellis couldn't help from saying out loud.

The kid in the outer office shouted, "Knew you'd react that way. Everyone does. If you're like most, you won't be able to keep your hands off it. Personally, I can't stand the noise. So I'm going to step outside and have a smoke. Knock yourself out."

Engaged now, Ellis kept opening and closing drawers. As he did so, notes filled the air—mostly discordant noise. All the drawers were totally empty. No one had left anything behind. But his fascination with the musical desk was enthralling. Ellis sat in the chair and just kept opening and closing drawers, trying to see if he could actually remember which tones came from which drawer to see if he could fashion some kind of tune—any kind of tune. Then a thought hit him like a sucker punch. His mind immediately rocketed back to Baghdad when he and his squad were charged with clearing one of Saddam's many palaces. They had kicked in doors, overturned filing cabinets, swept any and all rooms looking for potentially important information that had been left behind. They thought they were done in one workplace alcove until Corporal Lee realized that an intricately carved Chinese desk was similar to one he had seen on his last R&R in Hong Kong. In addition to the beauty and symmetry with which that desk was put together, it contained more than one secret compartment that would have been impossible to find had the shopkeeper not pointed them out to the Asian American soldier. Lee didn't purchase it, but he got a quick history lesson on hidden sections in expensive desks, which made it possible for him to show Ellis where secret drawers might be located in the desk they were searching. The squad wound up leaving with deployment plans they would have missed were it not for the knowledge Corporal Lee passed on to Ellis.

What might have been missed here, the P. I. asked himself.

The phone rang. Iris answered it. "This is Mr. Brownstein's office."

"Ms. Stanton, this is Brig Ellis. Thanks for getting me into Mr. Dane's old offices."

"That's quite all right, Mr. Ellis. Was there something else?"

"Yes, there is one thing I have to ask you about."

"Well, as I said, I haven't been back to those particular offices since I took this position, so I'm not sure I can—"

Ellis cut her off. "It's this desk. This weird pipe organ desk."

"Oh, my. Is that god-awful thing still there?"

"It is."

"I told you Mr. Dane was a different sort of person. That desk used to drive everyone mad."

"I can understand that, Ms. Stanton, but here's a question. Did Mr. Dane ever become proficient with this thing? I mean was he ever able to play actual tunes or melodies?"

"Mr. Dane became proficient at everything he did. Annoying people with that desk was near the top of the list."

"But here's my real question. Did he ever play one particular melody or phrase a lot? You know, like Beethoven's Fifth, *da-da-da-dumm.* Anything like that?"

"Well… now that you mention it. There was one particular sequence I remember hearing often. Though it was always when I was at my desk. I never heard him play it when I was with him in his office."

"What was it?"

"As well as being an exceptional filmmaker, Mr. Dane was also a virtual walking library of movie trivia. He was always quoting lines from old films or whistling the score from this picture or that."

"Yes, but what about the desk and the music?"

"Oh, sorry. Yes, I often heard him creating the musical phrase from that Stephen Spielberg science fiction picture. Those tonal sounds that began a kind of communication between the humans and the aliens. What was the name of it? Oh, yes. *Close Encounters. Close Encounters of the Third Kind*, I think."

"I believe I remember that, sort of," Ellis responded.

"I certainly heard it often enough. Remember, it was when the humans were trying to make contact. The people and the aliens kept repeating a similar phrase to one another. It went, *da-da-de-da-daaa.*"

"Oh yes. I remember it now. *Da-da-de-da-daaa.*"

"Yes. That's the one." But why are you asking about—"

"Gotta go, Ms. Stanton. Thanks again."

Ellis immediately hung up. Then he started singing the phrase to himself as he repeatedly opened and closed drawers attempting to get the right tones in the right order. *Da-da-de-da-daaa.*

The young man came back in from his smoke break, took the less-than-harmonious sounds for as long as he could, then said to Ellis, "I'm going to take my laptop outside. Just let me know when you're ready to go so I can lock up."

Ellis didn't answer. He was engrossed in trying to put the right musical notes together. Half an hour later, two things happened that jolted him back to reality. The first was, he got the notes right. *Da-da-de-da-daaa.* The second was, a secret compartment unlocked itself from beneath the desktop, dropped down, and opened. Ellis listened intently and looked around to see if the young man was still in the outside office. Then he remembered that the youth excused himself to get away from the pipe organ caterwauling. He slowly pulled the hinged compartment forward and looked inside. It was full of envelopes, computer disks, and thumb drives. After filling his pockets with the contents of the compartment, he pushed it back into place where it closed and locked itself. Still alone, he maneuvered the drawers once again to make sure he remembered the correct sequence. *Da-da-de-da-daaa.* It opened again. He put it back in place, now devoid of its contents.

Walking outside, he thanked the young man for being patient with him, got in his car with pockets full, and drove back to the hotel. At this point, he had no way of knowing whether the purloined contents of the secret compartment would have any probative value or not, but he was looking forward to finding out.

CHAPTER 5

Before the murder...

IT WAS A SMALL BUNGALOW, just under two thousand square feet, one story with a walled-in patio in the back. Of course, because it was in Santa Monica, it would list at about a million-five. Sam Brady had come close to listing it many times. He bought it just after his script for *A Cold Night in August* had won the Academy Award and he was flush with both cash and offers. But the life of a screenwriter in Hollywood is like a drowning victim, up one moment, down the next. One hit or one flop away from riding in on a wave or taking residence on the ocean floor.

Sam was in his sixties, which made him virtually a dinosaur to the people he was trying to work with or sell to. His hairline had already made a strategic retreat to the middle of his skull but that didn't keep him from wearing what was left of his coif over his ears and down the back of his neck. His mustache turned down on the sides and was as dated as his corduroy jackets and their elbow patches. But Sam never tried to be on the cutting edge of fashion or any other contemporary trends. He harbored the deluded impression that there was some value in being true to one's self, which was still probably the case in his hometown of Traverse City, Michigan, but was of no particular usefulness as a current inhabitant of La-La Land.

It was five in the afternoon and Sam believed that made it more than appropriate to supplement his Camel cigarette with two fingers of Woodford Reserve Kentucky Bourbon. He felt the need to steel himself for the potential maelstrom that was to come. There was always one storm or another that erupted when he got knee-deep in a script conference with Abel Dane, and his director was due to arrive shortly. The whiskey, Sam's first of the day, coated his throat with the flavor of oak and smoothly warmed his stomach. If history was any judge, and it almost always was, this first drink wouldn't be his last.

Abel knocked. Pounded is probably more precise.

Opening the door, Sam said, "I do have a doorbell you know, Abel."

The director strode in without being asked and headed for Sam's study in the back of the house. It was where they always worked when Sam wasn't summoned to Abel's office at the studio. French doors opened onto the back patio allowing plenty of room for Abel's pacing, which he did a lot of as they debated dialogue, scenes, motivation, and more.

"Don't like doorbells, Sam. They sound like department store elevators stopping on the fifth floor and depositing me in the middle of home appliances or lady's lingerie. Any wine available?"

"In the fridge, like always. It's the Puligny-Montrachet you like. I'm thinking of expensing it."

"Cost of doing business, Sam. You can't expect me to come over here and work without benefit of a glass or two."

"You mean a bottle or two."

"Always quibbling about specifics, aren't you Sam?"

"It's what writers do."

"Often to their detriment, my friend. Whether they'll admit it or not."

After securing a long-stemmed glass and filling it half-full, Abel joined Sam at the rough-hewn table they always used. A re-filled tumbler of whiskey sat in front of Sam ready to serve as crossing guard or co-conspirator. Enough of these sessions had transpired that neither individual felt the need for opening pleasantries so Abel jumped right in.

"It's the confession scene, Sam. It's just too damn long."

"It's not too long. It's the axis of the movie. The whole picture turns on what Miranda tells Kurt."

"The picture turns on the fact that Kurt finds out the love of his life has been banging his mortal enemy."

"That's what I said. And surely you agree, if the scene is going to be at all credible, it's going to take some time for Miranda to admit that. She has to get through oceans of self-loathing, guilt, and fear. Certainly shame that she let herself do it. Remorse for lying to Kurt all this time. And terror... that by telling the truth she may never see him again."

"That's how she gets through it in a book, Sam. Not in a movie."

"Abel we've had this argument before."

"And obviously you haven't learned anything from those rows."

Sam simply takes a swig of his whisky. Abel stands, glass in hand, and begins to pace.

"Movies are moving pictures, Sam, not novels, not stories, not even stage plays. It's not necessary, and in fact, it's not even professional in this day and age to give voice to every single emotion that arises. Less is more, Sam. Less is more. Don't have the damn girl prattle on and on about how sorry she is, how guilty she feels, how she's so afraid of losing him."

"You think it could be done with fewer words?"

"I think it could be done with no words."

"What the hell are you talking about, Abel?"

The director had finished his glass of wine and was pouring another.

"I'm talking about acting, Sam. That's what I'm talking about. Here's an example of what I mean. After a full day of shooting on *Shane*, one of the greatest westerns ever, when Alan Ladd was asked if he did anything worthwhile on the set that day, you know what he said?"

"He said I shot Jack Palance."

"Very funny, Sam. Very funny. No, that wasn't what he said. What he said was, 'I gave 'em a look.' A look, Sam. A look that said everything more eloquently than any speech ever could."

"If we aren't definitive, Abel, the audience won't be—"

"We'll be definitive as hell, Sam. We'll have Kurt simply ask, 'But Miranda, why can't you come with me?' And Miranda will give him a look. A look that spells out shame, guilt, remorse, and terror like no tsunami of words ever could."

Turning his tumbler in his hand, Sam responded. "Abel, I know I don't say this sort of thing very often, but I have to tell you. I really think this may be the best damn scene I've ever written."

"I know you think that, Sam. And you know what? You might even be right. It might be the best damn scene you've ever written. But nobody gives a shit about that. Not me. Not the audience. You think the people who buy tickets are coming to see what *you've* done? You think we should promote this film as the best thing Sam Brady's ever written.

Nobody cares, Sam. They care about the stars. They like seeing them. They're pretty to look at. They care about the story. They want it to be interesting enough to hold their attention. The truth, Sam, is that most of the people are going to come to this film because it's another Abel Dane picture. They're coming to see what I'm going to do. That's why I'm making ten million dollars to direct this thing and you're making a few paltry thousand to write it. That's assuming, of course, you don't wind up getting yourself replaced."

"Abel, I've got a contract for this picture."

"So what? You think the studio would blink if I said our creative differences were such that I just can't work with you on this film? They wouldn't hesitate. Your ass would be gone in a minute. They might pay off your contract. You might get your money. But how long will that last? And where is your next job going to come from? I mean, if you're dumped from an Abel Dane film, particularly an Abel Dane hit, which I think this could really be, then all of a sudden, you're *persona non grata* in the industry. What then, Sam?"

The writer drained the contents of his whiskey glass and said, "Abel, how many times are you going to do this to me? I mean why do you even hire me for your pictures anyway?"

"I hire you, Sam, because you are a damned good writer. A writer who gives me clay I can mold into first-rate films."

"But molding that clay takes a hell of a lot out of me, Abel."

"Oh, excuse me," Abel mocked. "Let me get out my violin. It's such a shame that you have to put up with philistines who don't understand your talent. I'm sorry that you have to subjugate your superior intelligence to troglodytes like me. It's terrible that you have to exist out here in the California sunshine from one day to the next, when you could be back in East Bumfuck, Michigan, turning out restaurant columns for the weekly newspaper. Is that what you want, Sam? Is that really what you want?"

"You know it's not, Abel. You know that I just want to do the best work I can."

"I do know that, Sam. And you can continue doing your best work for me. I'll just improve it from time to time. Like we're doing now."

"But for how long, Abel? How long am I going to be forced to be your indentured servant?"

Abel poured himself a third glass of wine. "For as long as I say, Sam. For as long as I can get help financing my pictures because an Oscar-winning writer like Sam Brady has agreed to come on board. And you'll continue to come on board, won't you, Sam? Yes. I think you will… because we both know the truth about that Academy Award you picked up for *A Cold Day in August*, don't we Sam? So, what do you say we move on to the denouement? I think it needs a lot of work."

CHAPTER 6

ELLIS EMPTIED THE CONTENTS OF his pockets on the desk in his hotel room. He went for the softer target first and opened one of the envelopes. Inside were photographs— nude photographs of Iris Stanton.

I'll be damned, Ellis said to himself. *The brilliant director... and his personal assistant... were perhaps a lot more personal than she let on. Of course, I'm jumping to the conclusion that he took these photos. Maybe he didn't. Maybe he just procured them somewhere from someone. Still, he did have them hidden away. Must have had a reason why. I wonder if she knew he had them. Hard to believe a guy like that wouldn't send out vibes to those he worked with, particularly people who worked for him. Yet, she hadn't had one bad word to say about the guy. Of course, according to the files, none of the five people who had stayed at the hotel that night had trashed him in any way.*

Respectful of the dead, Ellis pondered, or a sweep of potential motives under the rug? Perhaps some of the other contents of the secret compartment would help answer that. He was about to examine more of them when the phone rang.

"Hello."

"Hello, Mr. Ellis? This is Iris Stanton."

"Oh. Hi Ms. Stanton," Ellis said as he dropped the envelope

on top of the pictures he had been perusing. Somehow holding them just didn't feel right while he talked to her. "Did you ah… think of something else you wanted to tell me?"

"Well, the truth is, I just felt the need to apologize. It was rude of me to set up a meeting with you and then dash away like that."

"Does that mean… you didn't really have some pressing business you had to get back to?"

"You're very perceptive, Mr. Ellis. It's just that after these past months, I thought I put Abel and his death behind me. You bringing it up again, well, it sort of got to me a bit, you know?"

"I know that's the first time you've referred to him as Abel, and not Mr. Dane, which frankly had struck me as a bit formal for someone who worked with him as long as you did."

"Like I said a moment ago, Mr. Ellis, you are quite observant. Anyway, I simply felt bad about treating you as I did and felt an apology was in order."

"Tell you what, Ms. Stanton, suppose we skip the apology, and I meet you somewhere for a drink. Something's come up I'd like to discuss with you."

"A drink? Yes, I suppose I can do that. Are you free now?"

Surprised at the immediacy, Ellis said, "Ah, yes I am. Where would you like to meet?"

"How about the bar in your hotel? That's where I am."

This time the pause was on Ellis's end of the line, but he tried to recover quickly. "Well… great. I'll be right down."

Hanging up the phone, he quickly put the photos back in the envelope, then he swept the other items from the secret compartment into the top drawer of the room desk. He was halfway to the door with the envelope in his hand when he changed his mind and tossed it back on the desktop. On his way down, he was thinking about two things. One, how did she know where he was staying? Two, Iris Stanton was a very lovely woman.

The dark wood panels and red lampshades of the Chinese-accented bar offered a welcoming retreat from the dying afternoon sun. Iris was seated at one of the smaller tables for two and Ellis approached her.

"Have you ordered?" Ellis asked.

"I was waiting for you."

"What would you like?"

"A Grey Goose Martini."

Turning toward the barman, Ellis said, "Two vodka Martinis. Grey Goose."

The mixologist nodded and turned to get the bottle on the shelf behind him.

"Well," Ellis began, "I was surprised to get your call. Even more surprised that you knew where I was staying."

"Mr. Brownstein has connections all over town. A call from his office can usually turn up all sorts of information."

"Do you feel odd being here? I mean, have you been back here since the events of that night?"

"No. I haven't. This is my first time. I admit it feels a little strange."

"Well, I appreciate you coming over. And as I said on the phone, there's really no need to apologize."

"Guess I'm just built that way. Hard on myself when I think I've been less than straightforward... or when I think I've treated someone unfairly. Someone who seems very nice and is only trying to do his job."

"Well, thank you. I try to be nice as often as I can. Usually, it's a lot more productive than coming across as some kind of tough guy."

"You definitely came across as the former, not the latter."

"Good. To your point about being less than straightforward, why did you feel the need to pull your punches?"

"What makes you think I did?"

"If you really didn't want to talk then, chances are what we did discuss was probably superficial, and less candid than it might have been."

"No one likes to speak ill of the dead. At least I don't."

A waitress brought the drinks, set them on the table, and walked away.

"Okay then," Ellis said. "Here's to a new beginning."

They lightly clinked glasses, each took a sip, and he continued. "So, is there, in fact, ill to speak of?"

"I'm sure the more people you talk to, the more you'll find Abel could indeed be difficult."

"Difficult as in… ?"

"As in demanding, intense, frequently selfish. Wanting things done precisely his way. Almost always giving short shrift to others' opinions."

"I sort of took it for granted that a lot of creative people are like that. Is that not the case?"

"Some are. Some aren't. But he could take things to extremes. Still, you can't discount his talent. He was very successful. And his pictures made a lot of money for the studio."

"And because of that, people cut him more slack for… what did you call it… his intensity?"

"Yes. I guess that's true."

"You said he could go to extremes. Did he ever go to extremes with you?"

"What do you mean?"

"I mean did he ever ball you out, berate you in front of others, embarrass you in one way or another?"

"He could be obnoxious from time to time. But I got used to that. I didn't take it personally. It was how he treated lots of people."

"Well, and I apologize for pressing, but how obnoxious did he get with you? Be honest. You're a very attractive woman. You two worked together for an extended period of time. Was he ever out of line? You know, the whole Harvey Weinstein sort of thing? Did he ever come on to you... sexually?"

Iris was slow to answer. She finished her drink. Ellis followed suit. Then he held up two fingers and signaled the waitress it was time for another round. Once those drinks were delivered, the conversation started again. Haltingly, Iris recounted Abel's sophomoric attempts at sexual humor and how he'd kid her about not taking herself so seriously. By the time she was halfway through her second Martini she told him about the sordid scene in his office with the models' nude photographs. But she avoided bringing up the session where the director asked for oral sex in return for a recommendation to Brownstein.

"The guy sounds like a Class A Creep," Ellis volunteered. "Why'd you work for him so long?"

"I truly liked my work, and the company. The pay was good. I didn't want to lose any of that."

"When did you start your other position? Working with Brownstein."

"Shortly after Abel was killed. An opportunity came up, it meant more money. So I applied for it. The timing just worked out," Iris lied.

"Listen, Ms. Stanton, I really appreciate you telling me all this."

"Please, call me Iris."

"Okay, but then you have to call me Brig. And, actually, I

think we better have one more of these. You might need it when I tell you what I wanted to talk to *you* about."

"Oh yes. I forgot you said you had something you wanted to discuss. Then, Why not? Let's have one more."

Once each was into a third Martini, Ellis began. "I wanted to ask you about the desk in Dane's office."

"Oh, yes. That damn desk. You called me about that, didn't you? But I'm getting confused. I thought you already looked into that."

"I did. And it turns out the desk had an unseen drawer. A secret compartment I was able to open."

"God, a secret compartment. How like Abel that is."

"And in that drawer, there was an envelope with photographs. Photographs of you."

"Me? What kind of photographs? I don't remember any photos being taken. Certainly didn't pose for any. I mean, Abel didn't carry a camera around with him to shoot people or things. Didn't even use his camera phone that much. "

"Maybe someone else took them, and he got hold of them some way."

"But I haven't had any pictures made. Perhaps they're candid shots that were somehow taken without my knowledge."

"It's pretty obvious you're aware of the camera in these."

"Really? Well, what kind of shots are they?"

"They're nudes."

"*What?* Naked pictures of me? You can't be serious! Why, that perverted son of a bitch! But wait. I tell you, it's impossible. There are no such pictures."

Iris seemed truly irate, yet confused at the same time. And with two and a half Martinis in her, she wasn't holding back. "You saw these pictures?"

"Couldn't be helped," Ellis said as gently as possible. "I

opened the envelope not knowing what I might find."

"You still have them? The photos? You have, them, right?"

"Yes, I have them in my room."

"I want to see them. I want to see them now," she demanded. Then she turned her glass up and finished her drink in one long gulp.

Ellis wasn't at all sure where this would lead, but he also drained his drink and simply said, "Okay. Let's go."

After giving his room number and an appropriate tip to the waitress for the drinks, they left the bar. Once inside his room, Ellis quickly picked the envelope up and held it in front of him. "You are sure you want to see these?

"Yes."

He handed her the envelope. She opened it quickly and began to look. First one, then another, then another.

"Can you tell where those were taken?" Ellis asked.

"No, but…"

All of a sudden Iris's sullen mood changed. She actually began to smile. Then she started to giggle. Giggling a little more each time she'd look at a different picture.

Iris asked Ellis, "How closely did you look at these?"

"I had just opened the envelope when you called. So I didn't really examine them or—"

"These are not pictures of me. I mean the head is mine… but the bodies aren't. These are fakes. They've all been Photoshopped."

"Can I—"

Iris turned the photos so they could both look at them together. "Seriously, look at this. Now, look at me. Where could I be hiding boobs like those?"

She pulled another one off the stack. "And this. No, I haven't changed my hair color recently. In either place."

"Well, I—"

"You'll have to take my word for it."

Iris began to shuffle through them faster and faster saying, "Disgusting. Fakes. All of them. Why would he do such a thing?"

"Maybe he had some sort of obsession with you?"

"Abel wasn't obsessed with anyone but himself."

"He never came on to you? Never suggested anything improper?"

"Not overtly. Not specifically. He made vile jokes from time to time. Even went out of his way to embarrass me on occasion. But he never put his hands on me."

"Perhaps he was planning to use these," Ellis suggested.

"Use them how?"

"To get you to do something you wouldn't ordinarily do. I don't know. You tell me."

"Maybe he was just more of a pervert than anyone knew. You don't have to keep those do you?"

"For now, yes. They're part of my investigation. But I'll be discreet with them."

Iris, who was already teetering between shocked, woozy, and pissed, asked, "Is there vodka in that mini-bar?"

Ellis walked to it, opened the door, and said, "There appears to be."

Pulling out two mini bottles and unscrewing each top, he said, "I'll join you… if for no other reason than to keep you from consuming both."

He set the mini bottles on the desk, retrieved glasses, and asked, "Want to mix that with—"

"No," Iris interrupted, as she emptied the contents of one bottle into her glass, and took a drink.

"When in Rome," Ellis commented, following suit. "Maybe

you should have a seat first." He was about to pull out the desk chair but Iris had already plopped on the edge of the bed. Her initial anger had been followed by disgust, resignation of a sort, sadness, and eventually, tears that wet each of her cheeks.

"How could anyone do this? She asked, again bringing her drink to her lips.

"I'd say it takes someone who has very little regard for other people," Ellis answered.

"That was Abel, all right. But it isn't you, is it?"

Bringing her glass to her lips again, she slowly took a drink and said, "I mean, you wouldn't do something awful like that. You never would. I can tell. I could tell from the first time I met you. That's why I wanted to see you again, to give you more insight into Abel. But you've given me the insight, haven't you? You've shown me what an incredible bastard he really was. More of a bastard than even I knew."

"We all get blindsided from time to time," Ellis responded. "We can never know completely what people are like." Then he took his handkerchief from his breast pocket and dabbed a tear from each of her eyes before offering it to her.

"Can I have another one of these?" she asked, lifting her empty glass."

"Would you rather have something to eat first?" He asked.

"No. I think right now, this is about the only thing I could keep down."

He got another mini bottle for each of them. Then they started talking about Dane, but before she knew it, Iris was talking about herself. Who she was. Where she came from. Why she had always loved the idea of Hollywood and the movies and so wanted to be part of it all. Ellis listened, as best one can after the equivalent of five drinks and no food.

Both should have seen it coming, but neither could keep it

from happening. She was consumed with a need to be held. He felt compelled to comfort her. She wanted reaffirmation as a human being, not just as an image in a sleazy photograph. He wanted to treat her as a person, not just a suspect. She was a woman. He was a man. Even though both had more than enough reasons for restraint—emotion, alcohol, opportunity, and circumstance did them in. They wound up locked in each other's embrace, until exhaustion eventually enveloped them both with the balm of palliative sleep.

Two hours later Ellis awoke with a bitch of a headache, but without Iris, the envelope, or the photographs. He opened the desk drawer and was relieved to see that the other items were still there. Apparently it hadn't occurred to her that there might be something more than photos involved. Or perhaps she was just in too big of a hurry to give it much thought. Of course, his own thinking was pretty clouded as well. *Why the hell did I do that? With a suspect, for Christ's sake.* He saw the empty mini bottles and the glasses on the desk, but his thinking was still too fuzzy to remember exactly the order of events that preceded what had gone on in his bed. One thing was clear though. The envelope with the photographs was definitely missing, and if Iris took them, she had stolen potential evidence in a murder case.

CHAPTER 7

Before the murder...

NATE 'N' AL'S WAS THE Jewish deli of choice in Beverly Hills. It had been that for over seventy years. If you were going to talk about the movie business over breakfast, you talked about it over Nate 'n' Al's scrambled eggs and corn beef, or lox and bagels. And of course, lots and lots of coffee.

Abel Dane had arranged to meet Zack Richards at Nate 'n' Al's to convince him to take the lead in Abel's upcoming film. It would take a lot of convincing. Zack was the hottest leading man in Tinsel Town. Everybody was after him. His last three pictures had grossed hundreds of millions worldwide. He was the star everyone wanted and could have his pick of any role in or out of town. Abel was convinced Zack would not only be perfect for his picture, but also that the actor's stratospheric celebrity status would guarantee the film's success. Still, he waited outside the deli in his car for Richards to arrive. He was Abel Dane after all, and he didn't want to be seen sitting and waiting for anyone. People waited on him. No matter who they were. At least that's the way Abel saw it.

Richards approached the deli on foot. At that time of the morning, he had no desire to mingle with the masses, sign autographs, or be asked to pose for selfies with fans. Zack's signature wavy hair was covered with a Dodgers baseball cap. Aviator sunglass kept his sky blue eyes from being noticed by passersby. The collar of his leather jacket was turned up even though the morning was mild. Faded chinos fell over a pair of old Sketchers to round out the ensemble he often wore to avoid unwanted attention. Abel however, had a discerning eye. He immediately spotted the actor for who he was. So he waited and watched while the actor took both hands and used his fingers to absentmindedly brush away nothing that was under his nose. Nothing that was still there now. Zack went inside, then Abel followed him in just as the waitress was seating the star in an empty booth toward the back of the busy eatery.

"Abel," Zack said without standing, as he saw the director approaching his table. "I just ordered some coffee."

"I know," Abel replied, sliding in opposite the actor but not offering a handshake. "I caught her on the way and did the same."

"Great. So how have you been?"

"Busy. Very busy. Though perhaps not as busy as you."

The young actor once again cleared seemingly nothing from beneath his nose and above his upper lip. When he noticed the director looking at him, he said, "Just fighting a bit of a cold, you know. And yes, things have definitely been going well. I certainly can't complain."

"Guess not. How much did that thriller make?"

"A shitload," Zack replied. "That's about as specific as I can be. Other people keep up with the actual numbers, you know."

"I do indeed. Have a few of those people myself. Leaves you and me to do the actual work we love, right?"

The waitress arrived before the actor could reply. She set a cup of coffee in front of each one and asked, "You two know what you want to eat?"

"Give us a moment if you will, love," Abel said. "It might take us a minute or two."

The waitress spun on her heel and was off to another table without comment.

As Zack was dosing his coffee with both sweetener and cream, Abel was taking a sip of his the way he liked it, hot and black. Then he cut to the chase.

"So, what did you think of the script?"

"Think you have a potentially good one there, Abel. Tight. Crisp. Not overwritten. Shouldn't be that hard to film. Very few visual effects needed. Looks like one you can really sink your teeth into."

"Yes, but what about your teeth? What did you think about the role of Kurt?"

"Kurt's an odd name, Abel. I mean really, have you ever met anyone named Kurt?"

"Actually, I have. But that's beside the point. The damned name can be changed. What did you think of the role?"

Zack took a drink of coffee before answering directly. "It's a good role, Abel. A damn good role for someone, But not for me. Not now."

"What exactly does that mean?"

"It means it's just not the sort of thing I can do right now. Wrong persona, you know? Just too out of the mainstream. My people tell me I ought to follow my latest with a sequel, you know? Strike while the iron is hot."

"Ever get the feeling that your people might be full of shit? That they're thinking about what's in their best interest, not yours."

"Hey. Self-interest is what we all think about. You included."

"That's true," Abel admitted. "I always look out for myself. But that doesn't negate the fact that this role is perfect for you."

"Sorry, man. I just don't see it."

The waitress returned and freshened each coffee cup. "Ready to order?"

Abel answered without looking at her. "In a bit, love. In a bit."

"Abel, you can get this picture done without me. There are lots of guys who can play that role."

"Your involvement will ensure success. For both of us."

"It's not going to happen, Abel. I'm not doing it."

"What if I make you an offer… as Mario Puzo put it… that you can't refuse?"

"Gonna' put a horse's head in my bed, Abel, or are you threatening to have me killed?

"Not you. Just your career."

"What the hell are you talking about?"

Abel leaned back in the booth. He wanted Zack to see how comfortable he was with what he was about to say. "Remember that film you made a few years ago? When you were just starting out? *Big Boy*, I believe it was called."

The look on Zack's face was priceless—from Abel's point of view.

"How did you find out about that?"

"I have my ways."

"That wasn't even done under my name. There's no Zack Richards listed in the credits."

"The credits are irrelevant. It's pretty obvious that you are you."

"I have it on good authority that no print still exists of that film. It cost me an arm and a leg to make sure."

"You're right. No print does exist. But I have a pirated video of a number of the rehearsal scenes. The quality is much better than you might expect."

The air-conditioning in the restaurant was working, fine, but a thin layer of sweat was forming on Zack's upper lip. "Which ones? I mean what scenes are you talking about?"

"You know the one."

"You bastard."

"The one that validates not only the name of the picture, but your particular peccadilloes, as well... Don't you think?"

"You incredible asshole!"

"I really want you to do this picture, Zack. I think you'd be marvelous in the role."

"And I suppose if I do your stupid film, the video gets destroyed, right?"

"Well, I can certainly tell you what will get destroyed if you don't do this film?"

"Okay," the waitress interrupted. "You guys made your mind up yet?"

"Eggs are in order, I think," Abel responded. "I'll have mine with corn beef. Why don't you give my friend one of your sweet rolls? I think he suddenly has a bad taste in his mouth."

CHAPTER 8

OUTSIDE HIS WINDOW, STREETLIGHTS SHONE on Marmont Lane, letting Ellis know it was nighttime. Realizing he was alone, and not seeing the envelope or the photos on the desk, he remembered Iris had left with them. Ellis didn't think she would answer his call, but he tried her cell phone anyway. He was right. No answer. When the system suggested he leave a message at the beep, he did.

"Iris, this is Brig. Obviously, we both had a little too much to drink, and whatever happened... happened. If anyone's to blame, it's me. But, be that as it may, if you took those photos with you when you left, don't destroy them. They're potential evidence in a murder case. Just call me as soon as you get this message."

He'd try to contact her again tomorrow morning in Brownstein's office. For now, he wanted to examine the other elements he had taken from Dane's secret compartment. Reaching into the desk drawer, he removed a couple of computer disks, one thumb drive, and another envelope. When he turned the unsealed envelope upside down, a passport dropped out. It was a U. S. Passport for one Vadislav Zobeck. But the passport photo looked familiar. Ellis turned from the desk and picked up the police files that were on the bedside table. He quickly thumbed through them until he found the file on Abel Dane's cinematographer, Yuri Kaminski. Same hair. Same bushy eyebrows. Same glasses, nose, and beard. Same person. But why two different names? With no immediate answer to his own question, he set both aside, pulled his laptop computer from his travel bag, set it on the desk, and booted it up.

Once it was operational, he inserted the thumb drive he had found in the secret desk's compartment. It contained only one file labeled CDA Script. When Ellis opened it, he saw what he took to be a screenplay. At the top of the first page, it read: *A Cold Day in August* by Leonard Whitmore. *Who the hell is Leonard Whitmore?* Ellis asked himself. He remembered that he also had a file on the scriptwriter who frequently worked with Dane, but he didn't think that was the man's name. Checking the files again, he saw he was right, Sam Brady was the scriptwriter who had spent the night at the hotel when Dane was killed. In fact, Brady was the next person he had planned to interview after Iris Stanton. Ellis quickly raced through the film script, but it seemed to be just one scene after another. No comments. No notations. He'd have to ask Brady if he knew anything about it.

A couple of digital videodisks remained. Ellis slid the first one into his laptop. It was a grainy black-and-white video that appeared to be recording some sort of film production in progress. The picture started out a good distance from the scene that was taking place on the set. Then it was obvious that whoever was shooting the video was walking forward, eventually pushing past other crew members, lights, and paraphernalia. It came to a stop facing a huge indoor pool. Two pre-adolescent boys, wearing nothing but minuscule loin cloths, lounged on either side of it. Then from out of the water, a body began to emerge. It was a man using his arms to push himself up, out, and over the edge. He was the opposite of the other two, older, bigger, dripping wet, and totally nude. *Wait a minute,* Ellis thought. *I know that guy. I've seen him... Jesus, it's Zack Richards! His file's here, too.* But before Ellis could look away to find the file, the Adonis brought himself to his full height and began to stretch long and languidly, while the two young boys stood and walked toward him. The kids giggled and pointed at the star's manhood. He then stepped between the children, put his hands on each of their shoulders, and sauntered off while the camera zoomed in on Richards' retreating derriere with a small hand resting on each cheek. Then the camera that had been recording the event began to wobble as the sound of laughter emanated from its built-in microphone. It quickly tilted downward focusing only on the floor. Then, nothing.

Ellis was finding it difficult to believe what he had seen in the last few hours. Nude photos that had been photoshopped, one man with two different names, a screenplay by some unknown writer, and an incredibly embarrassing, perhaps even illegal, pirate video of one of the world's most famous movie stars. And he still had another DVD yet to peruse. He couldn't be sure exactly where any of this would eventually lead, but he knew one thing. Motives were stacking up like rush hour traffic on the Hollywood Freeway.

CHAPTER 9

THE NEXT MORNING, DETECTIVE ED Norman picked up the phone on his desk before it had finished its initial ring.

"Norman here."

"Ed, this is Brig. Got a minute?"

"Sure. Making any progress?"

"I wasn't initially, but I ran across something in Abel Dane's office that your boys missed."

"Why am I not surprised?"

"Don't blame them. The only reason I uncovered it is because of a Baghdad flashback."

"What do you mean?"

"Dane had this weird desk in his office. In addition to actually making music, it had a hidden compartment that I lucked into finding."

"And?"

"And I found a number of things inside that compartment that makes it look like some, or maybe all five of your key suspects, would not have been unhappy with a dead Abel Dane."

"Really? Good work, Brig. You're following up, right?"

"Yeah. As a matter of fact, I'm on my way to see that screenwriter, Sam Brady, right now. Do you need me to do a write-up or send anyone anything later today?"

"No. Adding resources now might only gum things up. Just keep me in the loop as you check out these leads. But shout if it looks like anything's about to break or if you think you're getting in over your head. In other words, don't do anything I wouldn't do."

"Well, that leaves the door wide open. I'll talk with you soon as I know more."

Brig decided not to mention the call he made *before* his check-in with Norman—the call to Brownstein's office that he hoped would be answered by Iris. It wasn't. A woman with an older voice picked up. She listened to his question as to whether Ms. Stanton was there and replied that she wasn't. She said she didn't know the reason for Iris's absence this morning or the particular length of it. She suggested Brig leave a number. He declined, thanked her, and hung up. Iris had failed to return his call from the previous evening. He got the same result when he called her personal number before trying to reach her at Brownstein's office. Zero for three. He didn't like that batting average, and he liked even less that Iris hadn't let her office know what was going on. Was she able to? Was something or someone keeping her from it? None of his unanswered questions boded well, particularly for Iris.

CHAPTER 10

MUSSO & FRANK GRILL IS one of the oldest restaurants in Hollywood, having served the famous, the infamous, and all those in between since 1919. It was where Sam Brady suggested he and Ellis meet when the latter told him he was looking into the Abel Dane cold case and wanted to talk to the scribe about it. Eleven a.m. was definitely ahead of the lunchtime crunch, but Ellis wanted to meet early because he had lined up another interview for later that afternoon. It wasn't too early, however, for Brady to have one of the eatery's signature drinks, a Bloody Bull—basically a Bloody Mary with tabasco and beef broth. It stood upright on the white tablecloth in front of him. With so few customers in the restaurant, it was easy for Ellis to spot Brady having seen his picture in the file.

"Mr. Brady, I'm Brig Ellis. Thanks for agreeing to see me."

Brady stood up, shook hands, and said, "Call me Sam, everybody else does. Would you like something to drink?"

"What's that you're having?"

"A Bloody Bull. They make a great one here."

"All right. I'll have the same."

Brady motioned for the waiter who came over immediately. "One of these for Mr. Ellis, here, and you might as well bring another for me." Then he turned back to his table companion.

"So, you're looking into the Abel Dane murder. Can't believe they never found out anything about that when it happened. What got it back on LAPD's radar?"

"Well," Ellis began, "some cold cases never really go away. They just percolate for a while until someone or something puts them back on a front burner. And the head detective on this one is like a Gila monster. When he gets his teeth into something, he almost never lets go before it's resolved one way or the other."

"You talking about yourself in the third person, are you."

"No, I'm talking about the guy who put me on this case."

"He must have a lot of faith in you."

"We go way back."

The waiter brought two drinks to the table and took away Brady's empty one.

"Cheers," Ellis said.

"The same," Brady replied, as each man took a drink.

"You're right, Sam. This is very good."

"Well, they've been at it long enough to get it right, I guess. So what's on your mind?"

Ellis answered that he had gone over all the initial investigative material and was just trying to look at things with a fresh set of eyes. He asked Brady about his relationship with the deceased, and the writer waxed eloquent for a few minutes, describing his relationship with Dane as both mutually beneficial and friendly.

"Interesting," Brig said. "I heard that you and he often got into some rather heated conversations."

"That's part and parcel of the business, you know. Writers and directors butt heads all the time. That's the way movies get made."

"How many of those head-buttings did you win, Sam?"

"Very few. There's a food chain in filmmaking, you know. If you're a director with the right chops, you're at the top. Most writers are generally found near the bottom."

"But I read about you, Sam. You've been quite successful. Didn't I read somewhere that you won an Academy Award a while back?"

"Yes, but in this business, it's less about what you did before, and more about what can you do for me now."

"What was the name of that picture, Sam? The one you won the Oscar for. The title escapes me at the moment," Ellis lied.

"A Cold Day in August."

"Oh yeah. That's right. Didn't see it myself. Was Dane the director on that film?"

"No. No, he wasn't."

"But you worked a lot with him after that film came out, didn't you?"

"Yes. We did a few pictures together. What's all this leading to, really?"

"Well, you see it's an odd thing, Sam. Some things have turned up recently that have begun to shed light on potential motives for Dane's murder."

"What sort of things?"

"I can't get into all of them. But one thing is odd, and I'm trying to get my head around it. You see, the other day I was in Dane's office and I happened to run across a thumb drive."

Ellis paused just long enough to elicit a response. He zeroed in on his tablemate's blinking eyes and noticed the taking of a good-sized drink before the writer spoke.

"And I take it, this is where I ask what was on the thumb drive?"

"Well, I thought you might know, Sam?"

"How would I know?"

"Well, I thought you might because a screenplay was on the thumb drive. A screenplay titled *A Cold Day in August*. But underneath the title, it said, 'Written by Leonard Whitmore'."

After another swig, Brady replied, "Leonard Whitmore? Never heard of him."

"You know, I had never heard of him either. But that's not saying anything because I don't follow the current film business. Mostly, I'm into older movies. Had a lot of time to kill when I was in the military. Spent it watching a lot of old films. But I digress, sorry. The thing is, I tried to Google this Leonard Whitmore. You know, there are one hell of a lot of Leonard Whitmores around. Though none of the ones that I ran across had any connection with the film industry. But it is odd, don't you think, Sam? I mean, that this screenplay had the same title as your Oscar winner?"

"You can't copyright titles, Mr. Ellis. There are tons of movies and books that have the exact same title."

"Interesting. I wasn't aware of that."

"Sure," the writer added, "if you wanted to make a movie about a bunch of pissed-off winemakers and call it *The Grapes of Wrath*, well, that's perfectly legal."

"I see. So you're saying that this screenplay, even though it has the same title as your award winner, is probably totally different."

Finishing his drink, Brady responded, "Sure. Probably. I mean, like I said, you can't copyright titles."

"You did say that, Sam. And you're probably right. But just to sort of clear it up, I'll probably stream your film tonight. It is on Netflix or Prime, or one of those services, right?"

"I guess so… I'm not really sure."

"Yeah, well, what I'll do is I'll watch it while I read along with this Leonard Whitmore screenplay. That way I'll know for sure."

"That's an idea, I guess," Brady mumbled. "But you know, anyone who has access to a Word document, well, they can change anything on it they want to. The script itself, the title, the author name, whatever."

"Guess that's true. But still, it's worth looking into. I say that because I found it where Dane obviously didn't want anyone to find it. Why do you think he had it hidden? "

"Beats me. I have no idea."

"Was Dane the kind of guy who might try to take advantage of something untoward like this?"

"Untoward? What do you mean?"

"Well, Sam, and remember I'm just hypothesizing here, was Dane the kind of guy who might try to hold something over someone's head if he found out that someone was taking credit for something he didn't do?"

"What are you implying?"

"Come on Sam, you're a quicker study than that. You see what I'm getting at. If Dane knew that the picture you're famous for was actually written by someone else, and he had a way of proving it... well, is he the sort of person who might use that to get you to do what he wanted?"

"Look, whatever the hell you found doesn't prove anything. Documents can be altered, like I said. And maybe Abel wasn't the nicest guy in the world. Nobody in this business is. But that... that..."

"Let me guess what you're about to say, Sam. You're about to say that doesn't make him a blackmailer, and that doesn't make you a murderer."

"Damn right," Sam countered, standing up and pushing his chair back from the table.

"Like I said, Sam, it's just a hypothesis I'm looking into."

"Well while you're looking into it, don't go around casting aspersions against someone's character. Dane's or mine. Sometimes all it takes is rumor and innuendo to screw up reputations in this town, even careers."

"I understand that, Sam. And I'm a discrete man. For now, our little discussion is just between us. But you need to realize this is a murder investigation and I need to look into anything and everything that might be relevant, particularly where motive's concerned."

"Yeah, well, your hypothesis is screwy. You could never prove it. It would never hold up in court. And I'm not going to sit here and listen to any more of it."

"What about lunch?"

"Ask for a menu. And the drinks are on you, asshole."

With that, Brady stormed out. Ellis stayed in and ordered the prime rib.

CHAPTER 11

THE SPRAWLING UCLA CAMPUS TAKES up a major swath of the Westwood neighborhood in Los Angeles. Westwood Village is chocked full of trendy shops, restaurants, movie theaters and more. On the backside of both the campus and the village is the quiet tree-lined street of Hilgarde. That's where Zack Richards' people suggested Ellis meet with the star. He was there to film a public service announcement warning people about the evils of opioids. The production company overseeing the commercial provided a luxurious mobile home for Richards to relax in until he was needed on the set near the UCLA track. A young production assistant escorted Ellis to the trailer and knocked on the door.

"Zack? The gentleman from the police is here to see you."

"Okay." Richards shouted back, "Have him come in."

"Step right in, Mr. Ellis. It's going to be about a half hour or so before Zack is needed on the set. I'll be back then to let him know, and to escort you to your car."

"Appreciate your help, young man. However, I don't think I'll have any problem finding my way."

"As you wish."

"*The Princess Bride*, right?"

"Sir?"

"Never mind," Ellis said. Then he thought, *Jeez, guess I'm older than I realized.*

Ellis opened the door of the trailer and stepped in. Richards walked over, wiped his nose with the back of his left hand, and offered his right. "Ellis, is it? I'm Zack Richards. Why don't we sit over here." He motioned to a plush leather alcove with seating that wrapped around a small table. As Ellis was sliding in, Richards asked, "Would you like something to drink?" He pulled open the refrigerator door revealing rows of water, beer, and soda bottles aligned in precise formation.

"Are you having anything?"

"Not right now."

"Then I'll pass, too. Thanks for seeing me, Mr. Richards."

"Sure. No problem. When I heard it was regarding Abel's murder, well, I'm happy to do anything I can to help. Though I'm not sure I can really add anything to what I discussed with the police months ago." As he spoke, he drummed his fingers on the table between them. Ellis couldn't help but notice how fidgety the actor seemed.

"I'm sure you told the police everything you knew at the time," Ellis began, "but recently additional information has come to light that we need to follow up on."

"Oh, okay. I can understand that. You know I played a detective myself in a film a while back. *The Devil's Handiwork.* Maybe you saw it."

"You know, I think I did. Pretty good, as I recall. About a child abduction, wasn't it?"

"That's right. Did it seem realistic to you? I always wonder if something I'm doing is as credible as it is entertaining."

"Certainly seemed that way. But I should tell you I'm not an expert. I've never actually worked as an everyday police officer."

"But, my people said you were with the LAPD."

"That's true. I am working with them. But it's really as a consultant. I'm a private investigator simply serving as an added resource," Ellis explained handing Richards his business card.

"This is a San Diego address. Why would the L.A. cops pull in someone from out of town?"

"Just a past association. Nothing more. Now, if you don't mind, I've got a few questions I'd like to ask you."

Richards glances at his watch, then looks out the window. Ellis doesn't.

"The film you had just finished with Mr. Dane, was that the only movie you had done with him?"

"Yes. It was"

"Did you know him personally, before you worked with him?"

"A couple of meetings were set up by his people and mine. But no, I had no personal relationship with him prior to the film," Zack said as he began to rock back and forth as he talked.

"How about the film itself? What was it like working with him?"

"Well, all directors are different, you know. Some like to give actors more latitude than others. More opportunity to experiment and try different things. Others are more authoritative. They know what they're after... and how they want things done."

"And Dane?"

"Definitely the latter."

"What about the other people who worked on the film? Ever hear anyone grousing or complaining about him?"

"There are malcontents on every set. But I never heard

any real bitching from anyone. Frankly, he was the kind of director who wouldn't allow it. If there had been any serial complainers, I think he would have bounced them pretty quickly."

"Can you think of any reason why anyone involved with that film would have wanted to kill Dane?"

Before the actor answered, he involuntarily pinched his upper lip between his thumb and forefinger. "Hey man, like I told the police at the time, I don't have the slightest idea. Nothing happened during production that would cause anyone to think someone might wind up dead."

"Would it surprise you to learn we've discovered some things about Dane that paint him in a pretty tawdry light?"

"Tawdry? There's a word you don't hear every day. But frankly, nothing would surprise me about anyone in this business. I'm sure there are lots of skeletons in lots of closets."

"What about yours?"

"What do you mean?"

"I mean is there anything in your past you wouldn't want people to know about?"

"Come on. I assume that's the case with everybody. Even you."

"Yes, but you see I'm not a suspect."

"And I am? Is that what you're saying?"

Richards then reached out with his hands, gripping the table to steady himself. He leaned forward and stared directly into Ellis's eyes. "Look… I was at the hotel that night. So were others from the production. The cops know that. They've known it since this whole thing started. I told them I was asleep in my room all night and I was. Nothing's happened to change any of that. Why are we having to get back into all of this now?"

Ellis began slowly. "Well, we've recently found that Dane was a collector of some rather odd things."

A look came across the actor's face as he moved back from his aggressive position on the table. It was the look of a man suddenly in no hurry to hear what was coming next.

"You know, in a normal conversation," Ellis said, "your next line would be something like, 'Oh, really? What kind of odd things?' But you already know, don't you?"

"No," Richards said, trying to regain his composure. "I don't know."

"There's this DVD. It has video on it that looks pirated. Quality's not great, but it's definitely good enough to tell what's going on. And what's going on is a young Zack Richards, stark naked, emerging from some sort of Roman bath scene. Then the strangest thing happens. But you know what that is, don't you?"

There's a reason stars are stars. The best ones are able to maintain their composure when everything around them is coming apart. Somehow they manage to stay in character. Richards apparently decided his character was going to be calm, cool, centered.

"You can't do anything with that tape. It wasn't obtained legally. If you make it public in any way, you personally, the police, and the city will be served with a lawsuit that will make the Jeff Bezos divorce settlement look like chicken feed."

"Dane let you know he had the tape, didn't he? Did he use it to get you to do his picture? Did he refuse to give it to you once the film was finished? Was he threatening to hold it over your head to get you to keep working for him on other movies? Did you figure the only way to get rid of the tape was to get rid of him?"

"Guesswork," Richards said quietly. "Nothing but one wild

guess after another."

"Well, we do have the tape. Plus, we have additional reasons to believe Dane was not above using things he possessed to leverage outcomes he wanted."

"What do I have to do to get that tape?"

"You could confess. Barring that, I'm afraid we're going to have to hold onto it for a while."

"I have nothing to confess, Mr. Ellis, and you'd better keep that tape under lock and key. I was not making an idle threat about your potential financial ruin."

"Oh, that's okay. The fact is I'm well acquainted with threats, idle and otherwise."

Just then the production assistant knocked on the door and shouted, "Zack? We got the long shot quicker than we thought. Can you come to the set now? They're ready for you."

"Don't let me keep you," Ellis said. "I think we're done for now. You have my card, so give me a shout once you've had time to really think about this. If you're straight with us, we'll do what we can to be straight with you."

Richards had no caustic retort. Nobody had written one for him. He simply rose, ran both hands shakily through his hair, and waited for Ellis to leave. The P. I. stood, walked to the door, and as he was exiting said, "See you in the movies."

CHAPTER 12

Before the murder...

TWO MEN WERE SEATED SIXTY-FIVE feet in the air on either side of a Super Panavision seventy-millimeter camera. High atop the Chapman Hydroscope Crane that held them, they could easily oversee the crew of thirty behind them and the lone rider they were getting set to film two hundred yards away. In a few moments, the sun would be in just the right place and the temperature at just the right degree to produce blue heat waves normally invisible to the naked eye. When director Abel Dane had wondered out loud about the best way to introduce the film's hero, his cinematographer, Yuri Kaminski, had suggested this dramatically grand entrance. Of course, that had been weeks before in the pre-production and planning phase of the film. Now that the shot was finally coming to fruition, Abel had convinced all of the cast and crew (as well as himself) that the composition of the shot had been his idea. This was far from an unprecedented occurrence.

Abel had been the recipient of innumerable suggestions as to shot setups and how to achieve them since he first began working with Yuri. Theirs had been an association that lasted over three pictures in a row—all quite successful. Abel was in no hurry to break up the team. Yuri, on the other hand, was trying to come up with the best way to propose a parting. He was appreciative of the opportunities Abel had given him. The director took a chance on him after he first arrived in Hollywood with only a reel of commercials and a documentary about Ukrainian fishermen. But he was growing weary of providing big ideas and getting little, if any, credit. Plus he knew of at least two producers who were ready to talk to him about directing. He couldn't get a swirl of ideas out of his head; being his own boss, calling his own shots, actually getting credit for his own talent and expertise. Such thoughts were so heady that the faraway look in his eye gave his mental meandering away.

"Lost in thought, are we, Yuri?"

"For just a moment, Abel. But only for a moment."

"That's not true. I've noticed you've been here, but really *not* here a number of times the past couple weeks."

"No point in discussing it now. We need to get this shot."

"The shot's ready. The sun isn't. We've got a few more minutes. What's on your mind?"

"All right," Yuri said hesitantly. Then jumped into it. "There's this independent film coming up. The producer wants me to direct."

"Direct? Really. Think you're ready for that?"

"You know I am Abel. I plan most of the shots we do already."

"Well my friend, there's a lot more to directing than planning shots. There's evaluating the script, convincing the screenwriter that every word he's typed isn't pure, fucking gold. There's battling the financial people to get additional funds to add a scene that was never in the picture, yet makes the whole damn thing work. There's ramrodding the crew. Not just getting them to do what they're supposed to, but getting them to like it as well. And what about the cast? Think you're ready to have an intellectual debate about motivation with some self-absorbed actor when forty other people are standing around with their thumbs up their asses doing nothing while you're losing your light?"

"Everyone has to start somewhere, Abel. Were you ready for all that when you began?"

"My God, man, you aren't comparing yourself to me, are you?"

"I may not have the experience you do. Not yet anyway, but—"

"Right. You *don't* have the experience. You also don't have the drive, the energy, the insight, the wisdom, the stamina, the ability to multi-task, the patience to put up with talentless posers, the... the..."

"The modesty, right? You forgot to mention modesty," Yuri snarked.

Abel caught himself before he actually chuckled. "You do have a sense of humor. Very dry. Very European. But a sense of humor, nonetheless. Now, enough about this ridiculous talk of directing. Let's hear no more of it. Sun's right. Let's get this fucking shot."

But Abel did hear more of it as filming progressed over the next few weeks. There was never another candid conversation about it, but the director found himself listening to suggestions from his cinematographer that frequently began with "Well, if it were me, I'd..." or "I think the best way to do this is to..." And these unsolicited recommendations were occurring more and more in front of crew or cast members, not in private parleys as they had always occurred in the past. Abel determined it was time to put a stop to it. Wouldn't be all that difficult, he surmised. Nothing a little public humiliation and private extortion couldn't take care of.

It was a half hour before dawn but the entire crew, except for the director, were already on location and preparing the first shot of the day—an exterior that would catch the sun rising in the east. The night before in Abel's trailer, Yuri and the director discussed where to place the camera for maximum effect. There was tacit agreement. So just before sunrise, everything was ready to go. Yuri and his team were taking a break and drinking coffee when Abel arrived.

"What the hell's going on here?" Abel bellowed as he walked to the setup.

"Nothing," Yuri replied. "We're ready to go. Just waiting for you and the sun."

"What's the goddamned camera doing here?"

"It's here because that's where you told me to put it."

"The fuck I did."

"Abel, this is what we discussed. This is what you said you wanted."

"This is what we discussed, all right. But it's not what I wanted and it's not what I asked for."

"Abel, let's step over here and talk for a moment."

"We don't have a moment. The sun's going to be up in twenty minutes and we're not close to being ready."

By this time, the crew was doing everything it could to look like they were not watching the scene unfold, even as they listened intently.

"I told you we were going to shoot from the top of that dune," Abel shouted.

"No, you—what are you talking about? We didn't discuss that?"

"The hell you say. How many times have I told you to take more notes, damn it."

"But—"

"Top of the dune! Now get up there and see what's required."

"We won't have time, Abel," Yuri said loud enough to make sure the crew heard him.

"We won't if you stand here jawing. Move!"

The sand dune was twenty feet high. Climbing it was not unreasonable, but the sand was so fine and loose that with every step Yuri made, he sank up to his knees. By the time he got to the top, he was breathing heavily, and he hadn't even carried any equipment with him as his crew would have to do. Looking down, he yelled, "Abel, this is not going to work. If we're going to see the actor's faces we'll need filler light, but we'll never get the brutes up here in time.

The crew was eyeing both of them warily now, would they go for the shot, or stand down?

"Use the damn reflectors, then!" Abel shouted.

"There won't be enough light," Yuri repeated.

"Do it, goddammit! Who's directing this picture?"

The next minutes were filled with grips, electricians, and anyone else with free hands tearing down one setup and scurrying up and down the dune to set up the shot before the sun tipped the horizon. Everyone was double-timing back and forth carrying the camera, cases with lenses, tripods, film cans, and more. It looked like a Max Sennett Keystone Cops' silent film with everyone dashing about frantically while one individual slowly walked up the dune to take his place at the top of the melee. Finally, with every crew member's chest heaving, tongues hanging out, and hands resting on hips to steady themselves, Abel turned to Yuri and said, "Okay. Let's shoot it."

"We can shoot it," Yuri said, "but when you see no definition in the dailies, don't blame me."

The slightest snicker snaked through the crew. But it ended abruptly when Abel sounded off.

"That's excellent. Fucking excellent. Then we'll just have to get this shot tomorrow morning. Break it all down and move to the next setup. And next time take fucking notes!"

Yuri knew there was no point in responding. He turned to his crew and said simply, "Next setup. Let's move."

The rest of the filming that day went relatively well. Shots that had been planned were achieved. No additional issues arose between the director and his cinematographer. Abel even asked if he could hitch a ride back to the studio in Yuri's old, but classic Porsche Roadster. With only two seats and the top up, the environment was perfect for an intimate conversation. Abel began it.

"Well, good day overall, I thought."

"After a bit of a rocky start," Yuri replied.

"An object lesson, my friend."

"An object lesson in what?"

"In the pecking order, lad. In knowing one's place."

"I know my place, Abel."

"You used to. Now I'm not so sure. All this talk about wanting to do your own directing. What could you possibly achieve that would be better than the work we're doing together?"

"We're not doing work together, Abel. Most of the time I'm doing the work and you're simply taking credit for it."

Abel winced theatrically as he said, "Oh, a cruel and unkind cut, dear boy. In the past, you would have never said such a thing to me."

"In the past, I never had to. It's only when I bring up my

future that things seem to get out of hand."

"Well, since we have this time together. Let's talk of both the past and the future."

Yuri's hands gripped the steering wheel tighter in anticipation. Though it hadn't happened lately, this wasn't the first time Abel had addressed his view of their relationship.

"Surely, I need not remind you that the only reason you're able to drive such a vintage car as this… is that I gave you the job that enabled you to purchase it. Or to make monthly payments on it, which is perhaps more precise."

"No, Abel. You need not remind me."

"And somewhere in that cluttered Ukrainian mind of yours, there must still reside the vision of me providing the one thing you needed in order not just to work, but to stay in this land of opportunity."

"I've not forgotten your help with the passport, Abel."

"Not just a passport, old sport. A work of art. The best thing the studio's art and prop department ever created."

"I'm indebted to you for that."

"You certainly are. It led to a Green Card. A second chance at life, as I recall you saying. You remember saying that, don't you, Yuri? Of course, it's Yuri now, but it was Vad then, wasn't it? Yes, Vadislav Zobeck as I recall. A pseudo-intellectual rabble-rouser who just happened to be in the wrong place on the streets of Kyiv during the Euromaidan Revolution. Of course, more protesters were killed than government officials. But when police are slain, as I believe at least thirteen were, well that raises hackles everywhere, doesn't it? I mean not just the Ukraine, but Russia as well. The Soviets are not fond of having their puppets ousted and their policemen killed. You know, even though it's been a few years now, I wouldn't discount the KGB's appetite for revenge. It's likely they still think of it as a dish best served cold. I bet they still have that interview with you on file. Plus the date and time you were scheduled to reappear for... how did they phrase it... more formal proceedings. Yes, as I recall, it was those impending events that lead you to look for safety in the good old U.S.A., right? Rather hurriedly, I believe. Without the benefit of a visa, or anything remotely resembling legal documents. Well, there was your original passport, wasn't there? The one I took for safekeeping while a new one was manufactured."

Yuri's head jerked involuntarily toward Abel, causing his hands to pull right also. The car veered suddenly, but Yuri quickly corrected. Then he stared straight ahead as he spoke.

"You told me you had gotten rid of that."

"Yes, well I intended to, but changed my mind."

"Changed it so you'd have something to hold over me, right? Something to keep me working for you whether I wanted to or not."

"I tend to think of it as something to keep you from making a big mistake. Something to keep you from taking on challenges you're not quite ready for."

"And just when will I be ready, Abel?"

"Hard to say, really. Perhaps after a couple more pictures... not counting this one. You see I've got a couple in development that I think we'd be perfect for."

CHAPTER 13

ELLIS HAD BEGUN TO WORRY about Iris. It had been a couple of days and he still hadn't heard from her. His calls to her cell continued to go unanswered. When he called Brownstein's office twenty-four hours after his first call, the woman who answered said that she was a temp filling in for the person who usually worked there. After explaining that he was working with the police, Ellis asked if a reason had been given for the need to hire her and the woman's answer was no. He asked if she had been told how long her particular assignment would last. Again she said no. Ellis didn't care for either of those answers. He asked her if he could schedule an appointment to see Mr. Brownstein as soon as possible. She replied that he was somewhere on the studio grounds at the moment and that she would have to wait until he returned to look into the possibility of a meeting. He liked that answer even less than he had the others. So he simply said he'd be in touch and hung up.

Ten minutes later, having secured Iris's home address from her file, Ellis was on his way to her residence, The Villa Bonita on Hillcrest Avenue. The place was straight out of the golden age of Hollywood, seven stories of white stucco with vines growing up the side of the building leading to its name emblazoned in black script near the top of one corner. It appeared to be one of those buildings that had been there forever and had managed to maintain its character while continually being surrounded by more and more modernity. Multiple ownerships and infinite remodeling had to have been done on the place, Ellis imagined, but he was glad that whoever the decision makers were, they had the good taste to pass on trendy and stick with timeless.

Finding a place to park was definitely going to be a problem, Ellis thought, until he saw a Lexus SUV pull out of its spot on the street and head for the boulevard. He quickly swung an illegal u-turn and slipped his sports car into the space with room to spare. Then he walked across the street and noticed that a groundskeeper was watering the bougainvillea near the entrance. One of the wood-framed glass doors was slightly ajar due to an electrical wire running from the workman's equipment to inside the lobby. Ellis never broke stride. He moved purposely past the workman and inside. Then he took the stairs rather than the elevator up to the third floor. Standing in front of 3B, he made one more call to Iris's cell. When she didn't answer he put his phone in one jacket pocket and pulled a Bogata Rake from the other. The specially designed tool turned the pins in the lock as Ellis slowly moved the device back and forth. In less than fifteen seconds he was turning the doorknob and entering.

Ellis found himself inside a very dark unit. A one-bedroom he surmised, but he couldn't be sure initially due to little or no light coming in from the outside. Drapes covered both the windows and even some of the walls around them. He walked to one window, pulled back the covering, and let light spill into the space. It revealed minimal furniture, selected, Ellis guessed, more for style than comfort. The couch, coffee table, chair, and end table were all art deco. As was the crescent-shaped dining hutch near the kitchen. All of it could have come right off the set of a Fred Astaire and Ginger Rogers movie, Ellis thought, as he moved into the bedroom and saw a four-poster bed in the same milieu. *Iris is living the dream*, he almost said out loud, *new Hollywood at work, old Hollywood at home.*

He continued scanning and making mental notes to himself. Bed made. Could have been the same day or sometime previous. Rooms uncluttered. Is she the housekeeper herself or does she have someone come in? Opening a door to a closet he saw clothes hanging neatly with bulky sweaters on a shelf above them plus shoes and boots below.

Moving on, Ellis opened the closed door to the bathroom. He flipped a light switch that revealed a black and white tiled floor, a chrome and glass vanity with a mirrored medicine chest above it, and the silver clawed feet of a bathtub just below the bottom of an opaque shower curtain covered with newspaper and magazine headlines from publications such as the *L.A. Times, Life* and *Look Magazines, Photoplay, People* and *Interview*. There's that confluence of past and present again, Ellis thought. He stepped forward to see if the bath itself was as spotless as the rest of the apartment. Reaching up with his right hand, he slid the shower curtain from right to left. The tub was neat, all right. As neat as one could be with a body lounging in a pool of water made crimson by the occupant's blood.

Finding a dead body is shocking anytime. Finding the body of the woman he recently made love to multiplied Ellis's shock exponentially. Iris Stanton was nude. Her wrists had been slashed. She had apparently gone calmly to her death. There was no sign that she had done any thrashing about, or bleeding over the side of the tub. Everything was clean. *Too* clean.

Ellis thought about the time they had recently spent together. A wave of sadness swept over him. Such a young life, gone. But he found it hard to believe it was really by her own hand. She never came across as someone with suicide in mind. Sure, she was upset with the photographs. Betrayed by what Dane had done and how he'd done it. But her main emotion seemed to be anger, not despair. She never telegraphed in any way that she was contemplating something like this. *I don't think she was*, Ellis said to himself. *And I don't think that will be too hard to prove.*

Then Ellis began to think about his options. He could report her death immediately to Ed Norman or others at the police department. Either way, he'd have to explain his presence there, and how he got in. Should he reveal his one-night stand with Iris? Who would that benefit? Certainly not Iris. Definitely not him. But what if someone found out later, or what if someone already knew? There was no way to be sure that Iris hadn't mentioned it to someone before her demise. Ellis knew he had to do something. So he made a phone call.

"Hello. This is Detective Ed Norman."

"It's me, Brig."

"Brig, good to hear from you. Anything new on the Dane murder?"

"There's been a development. One of the five suspects I was looking into is dead."

"Dead? Which one?"

"Iris Stanton, Dane's ex-Personal Assistant."

"How'd she die?"

"First glance would say suicide. But I think a closer look would say something else."

"What do you mean, first glance? How long's she been dead?"

"Don't know. Coroner could probably tell you. I just found her."

"Found her where?"

"In her apartment, at The Villa Bonita on Hillcrest Avenue, 3B."

"Did you guys have a meet set up or what?"

"Well, yes and no."

"What the hell does that mean?"

"No specific meet was set. But she had my card and I told her to get in touch with me anytime."

"So, she asked you to come to her apartment?"

"No, I decided to come over on my own. I'd been calling her cell and her office phone for a couple of days and hadn't been able to get in touch with her. When I heard a temporary worker had come on board to take her place, I got worried and decided to see if she was sick or something."

"Sounds more like something than sick. Did you follow up with the other four? And what about those things you said you found in Dane's desk? Any of them pan out?"

"I was in the process of checking everything out when I found Iris."

"Iris, huh? You guys were on a first-name basis?"

"She was beginning to trust me. That's why I think this is no suicide."

"Well, the crime scene guys and an autopsy ought to shed some light on that."

"How do you want to play this, Ed?"

"For now, I'll send a couple of guys over. You get out before they get there."

"What's your reason going to be for sending people over, psychic powers?"

"I'll just tell them I got an anonymous tip."

"Once your CSI team gets here, they're likely to run across my prints."

"Sloppy, were you?"

"I wasn't expecting to find a corpse."

"Well now that you have, beat it out of there. I'll have a cover story on the prints if they come up later in the investigation."

"Thanks, Ed. Guess we have both a cold and hot case now, huh?"

"Yeah. Just like running water. You think they're definitely connected?"

"Be too much of a coincidence if they weren't, don't you think?"

"It's been my experience that coincidences seldom are coincidences."

"Got two more individuals to follow up on, plus a little deeper dive into those things in Dane's desk. I'll get back to you soon as I do."

"Okay, now get out of there. I'll send over my guys and then I'll act surprised when they tell me what they found."

Norman hung up. Followed quickly by Ellis, who had decided to take one more look in the bathroom before leaving, but then he changed his mind. He didn't want to see Iris like that again. In fact, he hoped that image would start to fade soon, but somehow he knew it wouldn't.

CHAPTER 14

Before the murder...

THE RAVEN-HAIRED BEAUTY WALKED INTO the outer office. Stunning was the first word that came to Iris's mind as she looked up at the young woman who appeared to be somewhere in her twenties. She was wearing a short black dress with a plunging neckline that accentuated both her legs and bosom equally. Abel would be impressed, Iris thought.

"Can I help you?"

"Yes. I have an appointment with Mr. Dane. I'm Jocelyn Hayward."

Iris remembered scheduling the meeting, but she checked Abel's calendar anyway. It confirmed the woman's appointment.

"He's on one of the sound stages finishing a dubbing session, but he's aware of your meeting so I'm sure he'll be back any moment now. Please have a seat. Can I get you anything? Coffee? Water?"

"No thank you. I'm fine. I'll just sit here and wait."

"Okay. I'm sure he won't be long."

Fifteen minutes later Abel came through the door. He

immediately spotted the gorgeous brunette. "Hello. I'm Abel Dane. Sorry to have kept you waiting."

"Oh, it's okay," Jocelyn answered. "I haven't been here that long."

"Shame on you, Iris," Abel said. "You should have offered Ms... Ms..."

"Hayward. Jocelyn Hayward," Iris reminded him.

"Oh, she did, Mr. Dane," Jocelyn volunteered. "I told her I was fine."

"Good. That's good. Well, let's go ahead and step into my office then, right this way."

Abel guided Jocelyn into his office then turned to Iris and said. "Iris, it's virtually the end of the day now. Why don't you go ahead and knock off? Get home early for a change. I'll take care of this young woman and lock up afterward."

"Are you sure, Abel? I don't mind staying until you're finished."

"No. There's no need. I've got it covered. See you tomorrow."

Iris was less than sure this was a good idea, but she knew arguing about it with Abel would be even worse. "Okay. I'll pull my things together and take off. Thanks."

"My pleasure. Have a nice night," Abel said. Then he stepped into his office pulling the shoji screen closed behind him.

Jocelyn was still standing, unsure whether the director was going to sit at his desk, in one of the cowhide-and-chrome Wassily chairs that fronted it, or on the leather Le Corbusier sofa.

Abel dropped his shoulder bag on the desk and said, "Please, have a seat on the couch. It's much more comfortable. I like to keep initial interviews informal. Tends to put people much more at ease."

She sat on one end. Abel plopped down on the other, then

turned to face her resting one arm on the back of the couch and crossing his legs casually.

"So, Ms. Hayward, I assume your agent told you that I was looking for someone unknown for my upcoming film. Someone the public didn't already have an opinion about."

"Yes. Yes, he did. And please, you can call me Jocelyn if you like."

"I'd like that very much," Abel responded. "But frankly, you don't look like a Jocelyn Hayward to me."

"What do you mean?"

"I mean that I assume that's a stage name, right?"

"Yes. Yes, it is."

"What's your real name? You can tell me."

Hesitantly, she answered, "Maria. Maria Flores."

"Didn't want to get pigeon-holed into only Latin roles, right?"

"Yes. My agent said that I didn't really have a Spanish accent and that I'd get a lot more auditions if I used an Anglo name."

"But what if there were an opportunity for a good Hispanic role?"

"Well," she began, then immediately morphing into a natural but heavily accented tone, "I'd pump up the volume on my street lingo. ¿*Comprende, jefe*?"

"Excellent. An actress who can use her voice as well as her looks. Which are you most comfortable with?"

"Which what?"

"Which voice."

"Oh, actually the one I came in with. My Jocelyn Hayward voice. It's the real me, even though the name is artificial."

"Why do I think that's the only thing about you that's artificial?"

There was no mistaking Abel's tone or his look.

"I do my best to keep in shape. I know that's an important part of this business too."

"Indeed it is my dear. But rest assured it's not the most important part. If that were the case, movies would be filled with nothing but models. I refuse to cast models. I'm only interested in real actresses. That's why your agent suggested we meet."

"I'm so appreciative you agreed to see me, Mr. Dane."

"Please, make it Abel. Like I said, informal is best."

"All right, Abel. I've seen all your pictures, you know. You really are a wonderful director. Though, I guess that doesn't mean much coming from someone as inexperienced as I am."

"It means a lot coming from anyone, my dear. I've been known to take all the flattery I can get."

"Well, you certainly deserve it."

"I have a belief that we all get what we deserve eventually, Jocelyn. Though I must say that doesn't always put me at ease. You know what does put me at ease though, a nice glass or two of wine. And frankly, this is the time of day I'm usually having one. What do you say, Jocelyn? Join me in a nice Puligny-Montrachet?"

"Well… I guess so. I mean if you're going to have one."

"That I am, my dear. Happen to have a bottle in the fridge. You just sit here, and I'll be right back with a couple of glasses in hand."

Abel went to the kitchen nook. He pulled two glasses from a shelf. Then he reached inside his jacket pocket and removed a small tin with pills inside. Dropping a pill into one of the glasses, he then filled each with wine and waited momentarily to make sure the pill dissolved.

When Abel returned, he balanced the glasses in one hand and the bottle in the other. Then he handed her the glass he wanted her to have and moved the conversation to Jocelyn's past. He wanted to know all about her, he said. Where did she grow up? What was her family like? Who were her favorite movie stars? As the questions increased, so did the refills of wine. After several minutes had passed, Jocelyn began to feel odd.

"Oh, I'm sorry," she said. "I think I may have had too much wine too fast. I'm feeling just a little dizzy."

The bottle was almost empty.

"Oh, really? What a shame, dear. Just sit back on the couch. Put your head back a little. That's right. Let it rest on the back of the couch. Let me see if you have a fever."

Abel put his hand on her brow. "No. No fever. Perhaps you're a little tired, love. Let's just put your purse over here, and why don't you swing your feet up and relax for a moment? Just stretch out a bit on the couch. Don't worry. Happens to a lot of people who are stressed and have too much to drink too quickly."

Jocelyn was trying to say that she didn't need to lie down but somehow it was hard for her to form her thoughts into words and sentences. A bizarre numbness began to overtake her as Abel was slipping off her shoes and pulling her legs up onto the couch.

"I'm so tired… all of a sudden… so… sleepy… hard to keep my eyes… open."

"Don't try love, just lay back and close your eyes. You'll be fine. You just need a little rest. Happens all the time," he was saying as he ran his hand slowly up her well-toned calf, then over the top of her knee, then on toward the inside of her thigh.

Jocelyn had lapsed into something like unconsciousness— dimly aware of sounds and sights around her, momentarily immune to the touch and feel of Abel's hands.

He slowly pulled her skirt up to her waist and slid her panties down to her ankles. Then he reached inside her décolletage to lay bare her breasts. Standing above her, he undid his belt and let his jeans and underwear drop to the floor. Then he put two fingers into the wine that was still in her glass and followed that by sliding those fingers into her. Using his other hand to harden himself, he bent over and entered her, thrusting forward again and again until release came. Afterward, he put himself back together, then gingerly returned her clothes to the state they were in before she passed out.

Later, when she opened her eyes and began to vaguely make out her surroundings, she tried to quickly rise from her prone position on the couch. The effort sent off a shock wave in her head followed by a nauseous feeling in her stomach. Gripping the arm of the couch she sat up slowly and looked around. There she saw Abel sitting in his chair with his feet resting on his desk. He was smiling.

"Feeling any better, Jocelyn?"

"I… my head… did I get sick?"

"Oh no," Abel responded empathetically. "I think you consumed a little too much wine too quickly. Did you have lunch today?"

"I'm not sure. Maybe not. I can't really re—"

"Well, if you didn't, that may have been why you fell ill momentarily. But you appear to be all right now."

"Yes. I guess that's what it was. I'm so sorry. I do apologize."

"Don't be silly. You have nothing to apologize for. If it's anyone's fault, it was probably mine for offering the wine in the first place"

Jocelyn made an effort to straighten her clothes without making it obvious. An impossible task she gave up on as quickly as she had begun."

"Is there more you needed to know, Mr. Dane... I mean, Abel. Even though I'm not feeling particularly well, did you want me to read something for you? I could try."

"Nonsense, my dear. It's obvious you're not quite yourself at the moment. We'll schedule another meeting and I'll have you take a look at a script that's under development. I think there's a part that might be just right for you."

"Oh, that's so good of you. I'm sure I'll feel better next time. I really don't know why this came upon me so quickly."

Jocelyn stood, still a bit wobbly, bracing herself with one hand on the couch and wondering why she felt a bit sore where she did.

"Are you in need of a lift? Can I call you a cab or something?"

"Oh no. I'm fine. I'll just call an Uber at the Studio gate."

"You sure you're okay now?"

"Yes. I am. Just need some fresh air, that's all. Thanks again... Abel. I'll look forward to hearing from you... or my agent, I guess."

"I'll set something up with him. He'll contact you."

"I want you to know I sincerely appreciate this opportunity."

"Believe me, Jocelyn, it's great to find someone like you. The pleasure is, indeed, all mine."

She turned, steadied herself, and walked slowly out the door. He smiled, refilled his glass with what was left of the wine, and thought of what a pleasant afternoon it had been.

CHAPTER 15

ELLIS SAT AT THE DESK in his hotel room with a lot on his mind. There were still two of the five suspects who had been in the hotel the night of Abel Dane's murder that he hadn't interviewed yet, the cinematographer Yuri Kaminski, and the actress, Jocelyn Hayward. But it was the recent death of Iris Stanton that kept interrupting his train of thought. Had she really been killed by someone who tried to make it look like suicide? If so, why? And should the remaining four, who were at the hotel when Dane was killed, be the prime suspects in Iris's death?

Plus, there were still the items he had found in Dane's hidden drawer. A passport, ostensibly for someone named Vadislav Zobeck, who happened to look remarkably like Yuri Kaminski. And another DVD he was still analyzing. But he couldn't stop thinking about Iris. The woman he had held in his arms and made love to only days ago was now gone forever. He was determined to know why. Then his phone rang and he answered before it could ring a second time.

"Ellis here."

"Brig, it's me, Ed."

"Hey. What have you found?"

"You were right. The whole suicide thing was a setup.

The CSI team thought as much and the coroner's autopsy confirmed it."

"Give me the particulars."

"The team found traces of cleaning products all over the bathroom. Whoever it was tried to make everything seem spotless, but you can never get it all. And here's the thing. Even though her wrists were slashed, the coroner determined she didn't die from blood loss, but from drowning."

"Explain that, Ed."

"It appears the killer drugged her. There were traces of Rohypnol in her system. Once she was out, he probably took her clothes off, carried her to the bathtub, slit her wrists there, and filled the tub with water. Then he turned it off, tried to clean up, and took off. She must have still been unconscious but alive when the killer left. So her heart kept pumping and she kept bleeding, but she must have slid down into the bath, because it was the water in her lungs that actually killed her. With the drugs and blood loss, even though she was still breathing when she went under water, she would have been to too weak to do anything about it."

"Jesus," was Ellis's only reply.

"This was no professional job, Brig. Too many foul-ups. The botched cleanup. The drug that was used to knock her out. Nobody tries to commit suicide by taking Rohypnol. And here's the big one, we couldn't find whatever her wrists were cut with. No razor or razor blades anywhere. Who the hell kills herself, but somehow manages to dispose of the weapon she uses?"

"Why would the killer do that? Why get rid of it?"

"My opinion," Ed volunteered. "I think the dumbass got so involved in trying to clean everything up, that he threw whatever he used on her wrists, in with any other trash he took away. Hell, I wouldn't be surprised if he still has it around somewhere. This was definitely not a master criminal mind at work."

"Ed, has an approximate time of death been established?"

"Yep. Coroner says probably between eight and nine the morning you found her."

"Jesus. I missed it by only a few hours. I—"

"Don't beat yourself up. There's no way you could have known what was going on."

"I assume you've got people checking into whether or not our remaining targets from the Dane murder can account for their whereabouts when Iris... I mean Ms. Stanton, was killed."

"That was my next move."

"Have your guys look into Brady and Richards, okay? I can find out about Kaminski and that Hayward actress. Going to get with each one separately later today."

"Sounds like a plan. I'll let you know what my guys turn up. You do the same."

"Right," Brig answered. "Got a hell of a thing here, Ed. One old murder plus a new one. Maybe the same person killed them both. Maybe not. Maybe they're not even related. But somehow I doubt that. Hell of a thing."

"Hope you're not sorry I asked you to help, man."

"No, not at all. I'm just sorry about... Ms. Stanton. But somehow I think someone else is going to be a lot sorrier."

"Let's see to it," Ed said.

CHAPTER 16

ELLIS HAD MADE ARRANGEMENTS TO meet with Yuri Kaminski on the Warner Brothers lot in Burbank where the European was making a film. Ellis took the Coldwater Canyon road to get from one side of Los Angeles to the other to avoid the freeway and enjoy the twists and turns that put his 230 SL through its paces. At the right time of day with the right amount of space between cars, it's a road guaranteed to make driving fun again. When he arrived at the studio gate, the guard instructed him where to park his car and gave him directions to the "city street" where Kaminski was filming. On the way, Ellis passed a number of sound stages and a few extras dressed in costumes that ranged from cowboys to astronauts to aliens—the kind from across the universe, not below the border.

Ellis turned a corner and assumed he had come to the right place. Cement and brick buildings fronted both sides of a street that wound its way around a couple of blocks. Had he ventured into any of the buildings he would have found that they were indeed only fronts; facades that could become Chicago, Boston, New York, or any particular big city in any part of the world from any particular decade. Such is the movie's sleight of hand.

Long tables and folding chairs had been set up halfway down the street. Actors and actresses in what Ellis took to be 1930s or 1940s period clothes were in a long line with crew members. They were being served by individuals he would later hear referred to as craft services. There was a young woman dressed casually making notes on a clipboard near the line. She looked like someone who knew what she was doing so Ellis decided to ask for her assistance.

"Hello, my name is Brig Ellis. I'm working with the LAPD and I'm supposed to meet Yuri Kaminski. Somewhere here I believe."

"Yes? The police department? Mr. Kaminski's directing this picture. Everyone's broken for lunch at the moment."

"I see that. I assume that's why this time was chosen. Do you know where he is?"

"He and another member of the crew are going over a few things in the playback tent. Why don't I take you to him?"

"That's very kind of you. Thanks."

They walked toward the corner with Ellis feeling the need to at least make polite conversation. "So, is this some kind of gangster movie they're making?"

"You don't see people wearing clothes like those today, do you?"

"That's for sure. Is it supposed to be any place in particular?"

"Kansas City, 1947."

"Really? Guess it's been all kinds of places over the years, huh?"

"That it has, Mr., I'm sorry, what did you say your name was?"

"Ellis. Brig Ellis."

"Brig. That's some kind of military prison isn't it?"

"Navy. It's also an abbreviation of the word brigade. As well as a reference to old-time, two-masted sailing ships."

"Well, you're certainly a font of knowledge."

"With a name like mine, you get asked about it a lot. That's why I normally just go by Ellis. Saves time."

Rounding the corner they came to an area where a blue canvas-covered tent provided shade for two people, lots of equipment, plus multiple folding chairs.

Kaminski was seated in front of a monitor talking with one of the crew who had headphones around his neck, a leather case with a shoulder strap that held a recorder positioned around his waist, and a microphone in his hand.

"That's Gerry, the sound man," the young woman said. "They won't mind us breaking in, Yuri... I mean Mr. Kaminski, is great to work with. Very flexible. Not everybody in this business is, you know?"

"That's what I've heard," Ellis replied.

Reaching the two filmmakers, the young woman waited for a pause in their conversation, then said, "Yuri, this is Mr. Ellis from the police. He says he has an appointment with you."

"Oh yes. Thank you, Donna." Then turning to the soundman, he said, "Gerry, go ahead and get something to eat. We'll pick this up later."

As both Gerry and the young woman began to walk away, Ellis said, "Thanks for your help, Donna. Appreciate it."

"No problem," she replied, as she and the soundman headed back toward the lunch line.

Kaminski rose from his chair and extended his hand. Ellis shook it and said, "Thanks for seeing me so quickly, Mr. Kaminski."

"I was told you're taking a second look at the Dane killing, is that right?"

"Yes. That's one of the things I wanted to talk to you about."

"Well, I'm not sure I can add much. The police interviewed

me extensively when it happened. I assumed it was because I was staying at the same hotel the night he died."

"That's true. But occasionally, once time has passed, people are able to remember things that may have escaped them at the time. "

"I'd really like to be of help, but as I told the officers then, I was asleep in my room and unaware that anything had happened until they woke me up."

"Yes. As did the others who were there. But it turns out a couple have remembered things a little differently now than they did then."

Kaminski tried to hide the interest in his voice, but he couldn't hide the look on his face just before he spoke. "You don't say? What sort of things might that be?"

"Oh, things relating to their working relationship with Dane. What they thought of him both as a professional and on a personal level."

"Well, we worked on some pictures together. He gave me my first job when I arrived in Hollywood. I certainly appreciated his help."

Ellis decided to skip the formalities and cut to the chase.

"Mr. Kaminski, do you have a brother? Perhaps a twin brother?"

"What? No, I don't. I have no siblings."

"Do you know anyone named Vadislav Zobeck?"

The question produced the deer-in-the-headlights response Ellis was hoping for. When no immediate answer was offered, Ellis added, "Now would be a good time not to lie."

Still no answer. Instead a question. "How do you know of this name?"

"One of the things we found out is that Dane was a very secretive man who kept certain possessions hidden in his office.

One of those possessions was a passport. Care to see it?"

Again, no immediate reply. So Ellis reached into his breast pocket, pulled out the passport, and handed it to Kaminski who slowly opened it.

"Pretty striking resemblance, isn't it?" Ellis ventured.

Struggling to keep his thoughts together, Kaminski said, "They say that everyone has an exact double somewhere, don't they? What do the Germans call it... a doppelganger?"

"Yes, I've heard that phrase. Not sure I've ever really believed it to be the case, though. Aren't you also from Ukraine? And isn't that date stamp signifying entry into America approximately the same time you came over?"

"Well, similarities happen all the time, don't they?"

"Mr. Kaminski, we can get a court order and require you to give us your passport. It will be examined thoroughly and if it turns out to be a forgery, well."

"Look, Mr. Ellis... or is it Detective Ellis?"

"Just Ellis will do."

"I admit the picture appears to be of me. But couldn't someone have gotten a picture of me and used it without my knowledge... I mean that's possible, yes?"

"So, to be precise, you are disavowing any knowledge of this passport or the name, Vadislav Zobeck. You realize we can circle back with the Ukrainian authorities to see if this name or person means anything to them?"

"Mr. Ellis, I'm sure there must be some explanation for this, but at the moment I'm simply not sure I can be of any help."

Ellis reached over and took the passport back. After returning it to his pocket, he immediately asked, "Where were you yesterday morning between the hours of seven and ten o'clock?"

"Yesterday morning? What does that have to do with what we've been discussing?"

"Just answer the question, please."

"Actually, I was here. On the lot. We had an early call yesterday so we could start filming when the sun came up."

"I assume people saw you here during that time?"

"Virtually everyone saw me. The crew. The cast. Everyone."

"And you didn't leave the area at any time?"

"Of course not. I'm in charge of this production. If everyone else has to be here, I definitely have to be here."

Ellis plowed on. "How well do you know, Iris Stanton?"

"Iris? She used to be Abel's assistant. I knew her well then because I worked with Abel so often. But the truth is, I've barely spoken to her since his death. Didn't I hear someone say she got a job in the studio's main office? A good job, I think. Working for the studio head, Brownstein."

"Ms. Stanton is dead."

"What happened? She was such a lovely young woman. And a good person."

"Apparently someone didn't think so. She was murdered."

"God, how awful. But surely you don't think that I had anything to do with it?"

"I will find out about your whereabouts yesterday morning, you know."

"Good. Then you'll find I was telling the truth. I was here, making this film."

"Plus, I'll find out about the authenticity of that passport and whether or not any such doppelganger actually exists. Based on what I discover, you'll likely see me again."

"I'm sure there's some explanation for it, Mr. Ellis. There must be."

"I agree. There must be. And I'm going to find out exactly what it is."

CHAPTER 17

JOCELYN HAYWARD'S HOME WAS ON Belden Drive in the Hollywood Hills. Set high above Beachwood Canyon, it was a one-of-a-kind combination of nature and structure. Walls of glass on three of the four sides of the Mid Century masterpiece afforded excellent views of both the hills and the city of Los Angeles below. There was a wrap-around deck and even a Zen-inspired fountain perfect for relaxing. When Ellis reached the security gate he pressed the buzzer, waited just a moment, then heard: "Yes." The voice was a woman's, clear and strong, perhaps the mistress of the house, or maybe a maid. Who could say?

"I have an appointment to see Ms. Hayward. My name is Brig Ellis. I'm working with the Los Angeles Police Department. They called to set it up."

"One moment, I'll buzz you in."

Seconds later Ellis heard the automatic gate unlock as it slowly opened inward. He drove to the front of the house, exited his car, and walked up to the door. There he was met by one of the most beautiful women he had ever seen. Her black hair was parted down the middle and fell just below her shoulders. Full, dark eyebrows arched over deep brown eyes with natural lashes that curled upward. A short, straight nose led to a sensual mouth reddened by lipstick that seemed to glow. She was wearing red pants that matched her nails and mouth. A white peasant blouse topped it and the way her curves moved beneath it made it obvious they were unrestrained. He knew he had seen her before in one film or another but no titles came immediately to mind. Fortunately she broke the ice, keeping him from doing nothing other than standing and staring.

"Welcome, Mr. Ellis, I'm Jocelyn Hayward. The police informed me that you'd be coming by."

"Thank you for seeing me, Ms. Hayward. Hope you don't mind if I mention that in addition to consulting with the police, I'm also a fan of yours. But I guess you get that all the time."

"You can never get it enough, Mr. Ellis. So, tell me, what picture of mine is your favorite?"

"I'm not sure I could pick a favorite. I enjoyed them all. But that one set in South America... oh yeah, *Emerald Run*. Really liked that one. The action, the jungle, that scene in the lagoon where your face came up out of the water in slow motion. Very memorable."

"Well, I'm glad you remember my face pleasantly, Mr. Ellis. Can I offer you anything to drink? Coffee, tea, something stronger?"

"Nothing for me. I'm fine. But thanks for asking."

"Rather than going in the house, why don't we sit by the fountain? It's so peaceful there and the air is actually nice for once."

"Lead the way."

She did. Then each took a seat in small but sturdy wicker chairs on either side of a circular Japanese fountain. It was made of cement and sat atop a small garden of black rocks.

The water circulated through the fountain and the stones replicated the sound of a babbling brook and filled the air with a palpable sense of contentment.

"It's really beautiful, here," Ellis said. "I'm afraid the things I have to talk to you about may conflict with this lovely setting."

"Or, the setting may help ameliorate the discussion. Let's hope so. I was told you're looking back into the killing of Abel Dane."

"That's correct. And as one of the five people from the film who were staying at the hotel the night Dane died, I'm sure you can understand why we'd like to circle back with you."

"So, you're meeting with the others who were there as well?"

"Yes. In fact, you're the last of the five."

"And were they helpful? Did they recall anything differently?"

"Differently from one another?" Ellis asked. "Or differently from when they were initially interviewed."

"Either," Jocelyn responded, attempting to show casual interest rather than the intense curiosity that was running through her.

"Actually, a little of both. You see, I found a few things that apparently no one has known about until now. Things Dane had locked away in secret. Some of them helped jog your cohorts' memories, and some led to even more questions."

"What were these things, Mr. Ellis?"

"The particulars are not important to our conversation. There were computer disks, photographs, documents, and papers. Except for one, it was relatively easy to determine which item related to which acquaintance of Mr. Dane. The harder one was a DVD with a good bit of video, taken at different times apparently, of a small child. Little more than a baby, really. The video seemed to have been taken at some sort of child-care or school setting. Probably Catholic. Once or twice a nun will walk into or out of the camera's field of vision. It appears that the recording was done from a distance, as if the person shooting it didn't necessarily want to be seen. Occasionally it would zoom in to a close-up of the child."

"So… how does that have anything to do with me?"

"Well, as I said, it was obvious that the other items related in one way or another to the individuals from the film who stayed at the hotel the night Dane was murdered. So, I simply assumed that the DVD must have some relevance to you. Especially since the child has so many of your features—black hair, brown eyes, there's a definite resemblance."

Pausing before she spoke, Jocelyn said, "Mr. Ellis, millions of people have black hair and brown eyes. And lots of people look like other people."

"But few, if any, are as beautiful as you… or as angelic as this child."

"I'm not sure I know what—"

"Ms. Hayward, I brought the DVD with me. It would only take a moment for us to slip it into a computer. Then you'd be able to tell me whether it's meaningful to you or not."

"Is this really necessary, Mr. Ellis? I can see that it may have something to do with the Dane matter, but that was almost a year ago."

"Even though it's a cold case, it's still a murder investigation. And while I've framed this as a request so far, it could become more formal, and something that would need to be done at the police station."

Aware of the tonal change in Ellis's voice, as well as the specifics, and sensing she had little leverage at this point, Jocelyn replied, "That won't be necessary, Mr. Ellis. We can look at it here. Let me go get my laptop."

Ellis waited by the fountain as the actress went inside. He felt a bit like a tradesperson, not really of sufficient standing to be asked in. But he told himself he was probably overreacting. Up to this point, she had seemed nice, not necessarily full of herself like many celebrities appeared to be. Yes, she had been evasive, but so had all of the suspects he'd talked with regarding Abel Dane. Plus there was still the fact that innocent, guilty, or any place in between, she was still an absolute knockout. He knew he should put that thought totally aside, yet trying to do so was proving futile.

Jocelyn returned with an Apple laptop under her arm. Ellis gave her the DVD and she inserted it. As the video played, he watched her face as she watched the monitor. At first, there was no visible reaction. But soon her acting talent began to wane. Moistness appeared in the corners of her eyes. Her bottom lip moved almost imperceptibly. Almost. Finally, with both hands, she closed the laptop.

"Mr. Ellis," she began slowly, "if I tell you something in confidence, can I be assured it will remain that way?"

"You can be assured of a couple of things. One, I will try my best to keep anything you tell me to myself, as long as I believe it will have no immediate impact on the investigation. Two, I will tell you in advance if I have to disclose whatever you tell me. I'm afraid that's the best I can do."

"I hope I can hold you to your word."

"You can."

"Mr. Ellis, I believe the little boy in this video is my child."

"You believe? Surely you know if he is or he isn't."

Her tears had begun to flow more freely. She made no attempt to stop them. Ellis reached into his pocket, retrieved a handkerchief, and handed it to her. She accepted it and dabbed at her eyes.

"I feel that he is. I feel it with all my heart. But I can't say so with absolute knowledge."

"You're going to have to explain that one to me, Ms. Hayward."

"Virtually no one knows that I was pregnant. Most would have gotten an abortion, I suppose. Particularly most in my case; an actress about to embark on a real career. But I couldn't do it. I've been a Catholic all my life. I couldn't go against everything I believed. So, I went off the grid for a while, gave birth, then allowed the child to be put up for adoption. I was told he'd have a wonderful life. It seemed the right decision then. It really did. But after I'd made it, and he'd been taken away, I knew it was wrong. I knew he was *my* child, and that he and I should be together.

Ellis asked, "Do you know where this video was taken?"

"No. I don't."

"Do you know who might have taken it?"

"No."

"Do you know how Mr. Dane might have come into possession of it?"

"No, I do not."

"Well, pardon the directness of this question, but who fathered your child?"

"Why is that important?"

"In a murder case, everything's important until we connect the dots. So, who's the father?"

"I'm not at liberty to say."

"Sorry. That's not an acceptable answer."

"It will have to be. I can't disclose the father's name. It's a legal issue."

"Look, Ms. Hayward, I'm not a lawyer, but…"

"I can't divulge his name, Mr. Ellis. It was a requirement of the legal proceedings when I gave the child up for adoption."

"So… you *know* who the father is, but you can't *say* who the father is?"

"That's right."

"And how can you be certain? Were any paternity tests done?"

"They weren't really necessary."

"Because you were only with one man?"

"As far as I know."

Ellis couldn't hide the incredulousness on his face. "As far as you know… just what does that mean?"

Jocelyn had started to cry again. She did her best to stop the tears with Ellis's handkerchief.

"I couldn't really remember an encounter. Not for sure. Not for certain."

Ellis needed to reset. He said, "Wait just a minute. Let me make sure I have this straight. You realize you are pregnant. You are not sure how or with whom this situation came about. You agree to put the child up for adoption while also agreeing to not divulge the name of the father. Who did you make *that* agreement with?"

"The individual who paid for it all."

"And why would some individual pay to—oh, wait… I see. The individual who paid for everything is the father—whose name *he* didn't want divulged."

Jocelyn didn't answer. She simply continued her attempts to keep from crying.

Then something leapt into Ellis's mind. He didn't know from where. But suddenly he was remembering that Ed Norman told him traces of Rohypnol were found in Iris Stanton's body.

"Could you have been a victim of date rape, Ms. Hayward? Is that why you say you can't be totally positive about the father?"

"Mr. Ellis, please."

He began before she could continue. "Did you party a lot during that time? Go to clubs or private gatherings where drugs may have been easily accessible?"

"No, Mr. Ellis. I didn't. I was dedicated to getting my career off the ground as a real actress, not as just more Hollywood arm candy."

Quickly, Ellis started to replay all the things he had recently discovered. It was Dane who arranged to get pervy pictures of Iris. For his own weird enjoyment, or as some way to hold something over her head? Dane had secured the nude tape of Zack Richards. He must have had some particular use for that. And what about the Oscar-winning script of Sam Brady's movie with someone else's name on it? Plus the photograph of Yuri Kaminski on a passport for one Vadislav Zobeck. *Jesus,* he thought. *If Dane had something on all of them… something he could use to make them dance to his tunes… then why not Jocelyn Hayward as well?*

"Ms. Hayward, I know you performed in a picture for Dane. And I could probably find this in your file, but right now it escapes me. When did you first meet or come in contact with Abel Dane?"

"My agent got me an appointment to see him in his office. He was casting a new film and looking for actresses who were not well known. That was certainly me at that time."

"How did the meeting go?"

"Well," she began hesitantly, "it was okay, I guess. I really remember very little of it."

"Why is that? First time meeting with a big, important director. Seems to me like you'd remember it quite well."

"I think I became slightly ill in that meeting. Abel offered me wine, which he was having also, and I may have had too much too quickly. So I just don't recall much of what went on."

"And about how long after that did you realize you were pregnant?"

"Well, it was a number of weeks, but…"

Ellis couldn't think of a good reason not to keep putting pressure on the actress. So he charged forward. "Let me put a hypothetical to you. Merely something that is in the realm of possibility. Let's say you did overindulge in that meeting. But what you overindulged in was a date-rape drug Dane put in your wine. Let's also say that you winding up pregnant a few weeks later was a result of that meeting. Let's go on to say that you told Dane of your situation and that you had no intention of aborting the pregnancy. It's not totally unimaginable then, that he might have arranged for everything else; the birth, the adoption, and the legality prohibiting you from naming the father. Interesting hypothetical, don't you think?"

Jocelyn was no longer crying, but she wasn't responding either. She was simply staring into space with Ellis's handkerchief in her hands.

"After the child was born, did Dane—?"

"I can't talk about this, Mr. Ellis."

"Did he want the boy for himself? Or was he using him as a carrot? Something kept just out of your reach, so you would do whatever he wanted you to."

"We have to end this conversation, please."

"Or," Ellis paused momentarily, "did you maintain hope of one day getting the child back? Via legal means or otherwise?"

Physically deflated and emotionally spent, Jocelyn replied, "I have nothing more to say, Mr. Ellis. If you or anyone you're working with wants to speak with me again, it will have to be with my attorney present."

"I meant what I said, Ms. Hayward. About keeping what you've told me confidential, at least until it becomes something I'm duty-bound to share. But you do need to realize that the hypothetical we've just discussed certainly could be seen, with further investigation, as a potential motive for murder."

"I'm neither naive nor intellectually deficient, Mr. Ellis. I understand that quite well."

Ellis rose from his seat, but before he turned to go, he said, "I am sorry, but there is one more question I need to ask you. Where were you yesterday between seven and ten in the morning?"

"I was here. Why do you ask?"

"Can anyone vouch for that?"

"My maid, Consuela. She arrives at six-thirty every morning and leaves at four."

"That's rather early, isn't it?"

"She has her own key and lets herself in. You still haven't told me why you want to know?"

"Yesterday morning, Iris Stanton was killed."

The shock was obvious. "Iris? Who used to work with Abel? My God. How did it happen?"

"We believe she was murdered?"

"That's so awful. Do you know who did—oh, I guess you don't... or you wouldn't be asking me where I was at that time."

"We're going to find Iris's killer, Ms. Hayward... and Dane's"

Jocelyn then realized she was still hanging on to Ellis's handkerchief. "Why don't I keep this and have it washed? Then I'll get it back to you."

"Whatever you like. I'm just sorry to have been the bearer of such bad news."

"I'm sorry, too."

"There is at least one piece of good news I could share," Ellis offered.

"What would that be?

"When I said that you may indeed have a motive for murder…"

"Yes?"

"Well, yours isn't the only one we've turned up."

CHAPTER 18

SAM BRADY WAS HALFWAY DONE with a love scene and a second whiskey when his doorbell rang. He wasn't expecting anyone or anything so he just kept writing. The second time it rang, he lost his train of thought. So he decided he might as well get up and see who was at his door. When he opened it, he saw two guys in off-the-rack suits. His initial thought was that they were too old to be Church of Latter-Day Saints missionaries. He was right.

One was Anthony Russo, a short, stocky fellow with a ruddy complexion and a countenance that definitely looked lived-in. The other was Paul Jamison. Tall. Bald. Could have been mistaken for a nightclub bouncer if it wasn't so obvious he was a cop. They were both members of Ed Norman's squad.

"Sam Brady?"

"That's right."

"I'm Detective Russo. This is Detective Jamison. We're with the LAPD. Need to ask you a couple of questions."

"About what?"

"Mind if we step inside, sir?"

"I don't know if I mind. What is this about?"

"It's about a murder investigation," Russo said. "Got a problem with us coming in?"

"No. No problem. Come on in."

Sam opened the door wider, stepped aside, let the two officers into the living room, and closed the door behind them.

"This isn't more about the Abel Dane killing, is it?"

"Who's Abel Dane?" Russo asked.

"You know, the director that was killed a year or so ago."

"Don't know anything about that sir. Is that some crime you are connected to?"

"No, certainly not," Sam blurted. "I thought you might have just been following up on it because I worked with the guy a time or two. That's all."

"Nothing to do with us," Russo said. "We're here on another matter."

"But you did say it was a murder investigation, right? Who was murdered?"

"A young woman named Iris Stanton."

"Iris Stanton? You must be joking."

"Comedy isn't our line," Russo replied, "regardless of what you see on TV. This is an actual homicide."

"It's just... Iris Stanton... I can't believe it."

Jamison hadn't opened his mouth once and it didn't look like he was going to. Russo kept up the questioning. "So, we take it you knew Ms. Stanton?"

"Yes. I knew her. She's... I mean, she was Abel Dane's assistant."

"Is that the fellow you mentioned moments ago? The one you said was a director?"

"Ah, yes. Iris was his assistant for a while. She worked with him when I was writing a couple of his pictures."

"And you said somebody offed this guy, Dane?"

"Yes. He was murdered. But like I said, that's been almost a year ago."

Russo, who had now begun to take notes in his spiral-bound pad, said, "Let me get this straight. You know the victim we're looking into… Iris Stanton… worked with this director who was also murdered about a year ago. What'd you say his name was?"

"Abel. Abel Dane," Brady replied reluctantly.

"You think the two killings are connected?" Russo asked.

"I don't have the slightest idea, detective. But they're so far apart. Seems unlikely to me."

"When's the last time you saw Iris Stanton?"

"Saw her? Well, let me see. It might have been Abel Dane's funeral. But as I said, that was months and months ago. I think I heard that she got another job in the studio, working for the fellow who runs the place, Brownstein."

"That a first or last name, Mr. Brady?"

"Last. Don't ask me his first name. It escapes me at the moment."

"Know his first name?"

"I just said it escapes me. Hell, he's the head of the damned studio. Surely you guys can come up with his name."

"We can do that, sir. No problem. 'And don't call me Shirley.' Ha, remember that one, Mr. Brady? Leslie Neilson, *Airplane*. And he was in those *Naked Gun* movies, too. Remember them?"

"Yes, I remember them, detective. Wish I'd written them. They made a mint. Police didn't take offense at those?"

"Cops loved 'em. They were just satire, right? That what you call it?"

"More approaching burlesque," Brady responded.

"Well, whatever. They were funny." Then Russo added, "I mean if you can't laugh at yourself, who the hell can you laugh at?"

Brady's unexplained reply. "I've been wondering a lot about that lately."

"Sorry, got us off track for a minute." Checking his notes, Russo continued. "So you said the last time you saw Iris Stanton was a few months ago. But you're not sure?"

"Not exactly sure, detective. But I know it's been a very long time."

"Okay. So can you account for your whereabouts yesterday morning? Say, from maybe seven to ten?"

"Yes. I can. I was having breakfast with a couple of friends from the Writers Guild."

"And just where was this breakfast?"

"Amelia's at Santa Monica and Main. We get together there for breakfast a couple of times a month."

"You wouldn't mind jotting down the names and phone numbers of the pair you ate with yesterday, would you Mr. Brady?" Offering his notebook, he added, "Just anywhere there on that blank page."

As Brady was putting the information down, he looked over at the still quiet Jamison and said, "Partner doesn't say much, does he? Supposed to be the intimidating one, or what?"

"Not really," Russo answered. "There's a reason the department sends us out in pairs. He's supposed to do the looking while I do the talking and thinking. His job is to make sure whoever we're interviewing doesn't pull a gun, or a knife, or a long pair of scissors out of their pants, skirt, or some dresser drawer and take issue with our approach. You'd be surprised at what we run into now and then."

Brady finished writing down the names and phone numbers. Then he handed the notepad to Russo who took it back by the spiral top and dropped it in his pocket. A pocket that now held Brady's fingerprints.

"Can you tell me how it happened, Detective Russo?"

"I could, sir, but I'd really rather not at this time. Need to keep some details under wraps until our investigation is further along. But it wasn't pretty."

"That's a terrible shame. I remember Iris being a lovely young woman."

"The world can be a nasty place, Mr. Brady. Well, thanks for your time. We'll get back to you if any more questions come up. Take my card, here. And give me a call if anything comes to mind about Ms. Stanton… or that other fellow's murder you mentioned. You never know."

"You certainly don't, Detective."

Brady escorted the two officers out and shut the door behind them. When he did, he said to himself, *Jesus fucking Christ!* Five minutes later, he was on the phone.

After ringing four times, the slightly European, male voice came on and said, "Sorry, I can't come to the phone right now. Leave your number and I'll call you back."

"Yuri, this is Sam Brady. I think we need to get together. I know I said we shouldn't do that. But things have changed. It's important. Call me back and we'll set up a time and place. I'll call the others."

His next call was answered.

"Hello."

"Jocelyn, is that you?"

"Who is this?"

"It's Sam. Sam Brady."

"Sam? Why are you calling? What is it?"

"Have you heard about Iris Stanton?"

"Yes. I have. I can't believe it."

"How did you find out?"

"Some policeman came. Said he wanted to talk about Abel's

death. But before he left, he told me about Iris."

"Was he by himself?"

"Yes."

"A tall guy? Not bad looking? Say his name was Ellis?"

"That's right."

"You didn't say anything you shouldn't, did you?"

"He had a DVD, Sam. Said he found it someplace Abel had hidden it. I couldn't avoid it, Sam. He seemed to know so much already."

"What do you mean you couldn't avoid it? Couldn't avoid what? What was on the DVD?"

"Video of my son, Sam. Shots of him at the Catholic Center."

"Did you admit that Abel was the father?"

"I didn't have to, Sam. He seemed to know already."

"Damn, Jocelyn! What else did you tell him?"

"Nothing. Nothing about the rest of us, I swear it."

"Look, I think we should get together."

"But… you said at the time, we'd never need to meet again."

"We wouldn't. Except for this thing with Iris. There seem to be two different investigations going on. One about Abel. Another about Iris. Two detectives were at my place just now asking about her."

"Was Ellis one of them?"

"No. But he came to see me a couple days ago about Abel's death. There's just too much going on here. I really think we need to meet. I'll contact the others and set something up. Then I'll get back to you. But don't say anything more to anyone until we've had a chance to think this out."

"All right, Sam. I won't. I'll wait to hear from you."

They both hung up and Sam immediately dialed Zack Richards's personal cell phone. It rang multiple times. Then a voice told him what number he'd reached and provided a beep to precede any message he might want to leave.

"Zack, this is Sam Brady. Listen, call me back the minute you get this. If they haven't already, there are going to be cops coming to see you. Clam up, man. Don't say anything about anything. I'm going to arrange a meet. I'll call you when it's set up. But for now, say absolutely nothing, regardless of what you get asked. Oh yeah, and if you don't already, be sure and have an alibi for where you were early yesterday morning. You're going to need one."

CHAPTER 19

THE FRONT YARD OF A meticulously maintained, ranch-style home in Pacific Palisades was swarming with cast, crew, and neighborhood onlookers. Zack Richards was standing nearest the camera in the foreground with a central casting mom, dad, and two kids performing pre-rehearsed family togetherness in the background. It was the last scene of the anti-opioid public service spot the star had agreed to do and they were already up to the eighth take. Zack kept muffing the final line as well as the recitation of the phone number and the website to call for help, even though both were written large and held up on giant cue cards behind the camera. Everyone there knew his mind must be elsewhere, or he hadn't gotten enough sleep last night, or he was high on something. No one but Zack knew it was all three. When takes nine and ten were flubbed as well, the decision was made that while Zack was reading the last line, the camera would push past him to the family in the background, hold for a second, then slowly dissolve to a title card with the emergency number to call and the organization's website. Zack muffed the next two takes as well but managed to finally hit everything perfectly on take 13. Putting superstition aside, the director said he was satisfied and the shoot wrapped.

While the crew was breaking down the set and putting away equipment, Zack stayed just long enough to make one high school girl happy by signing an autograph, then pissing off the rest of the neighborhood by not staying to sign more. He had driven to the location in his new fire engine red Porsche Carrera GT, a car at this stage of his career that he could afford more easily than he could drive. But it had the look he wanted and that was what was important to Zack. It also had his cell phone, which he retrieved once he unlocked the door and dropped into the driver's seat. Checking his messages, he saw the recent one from Sam Brady and played it back. It had barely ended when he glanced in his rearview mirror and saw the production assistant standing by a car with two men inside who—even in Zack's drug-fueled state—couldn't be anything other than cops. The PA was pointing toward Zack's car. His gesture triggered an involuntary fight/flight response in Zack that was all flight and no fight. Turning the V10, six hundred and three horsepower engine over, he barreled away from the curb and spun down the street barely keeping the racing vehicle stable.

Officers Russo and Jamison couldn't miss the Porsche peeling out. Jamison was behind the wheel of the LAPD's unmarked Dodge Charger. He jerked the gear from Park to Drive, activated the compact flashing dash lights affixed to the windshield, and put his own pedal to the metal. In addition to an automatic adrenalin rush Russo felt in his stomach, something inside his cranium started signaling that this was not going to end well.

Barely missing cars parked on the streets, two bicyclists, one pedestrian, and multiple stop signs, Zack sped through three residential blocks and made a hard right turn to head west on Sunset Boulevard. In his cocaine-addled mind, he figured if he could get to the Pacific Coast Highway, then he could put enough space between himself and the two cops on his tail to lose them for good. Of course, it never occurred to him that they could call for backup and eventually have someone in front of him as well as behind him.

Russo and Jamison were doing everything possible to catch up, but they were only holding the distance between their car and his, not shortening it. Russo had, however, put out a call for assistance while Jamison did his best to keep up the chase without injury to anyone unlucky enough to be in the vicinity.

As Zack barreled down the boulevard racing toward the intersection where Sunset meets the sea, the LAPD already had squad cars converging on the Pacific Coast Highway stoplight outside Gladstone's beachside restaurant. Zack kept glancing in his rearview mirror to see if the Dodge he was running from was gaining on him. Each time he did so, the steering on the Porsche was so responsive that the slightest movement jerked the Carrera from side to side. Traffic coming toward him was immediately swerving to the right because it looked like the GT was some sort of wild runaway. The cars Zack was screaming around, both left and right, were doing whatever they could to get out of his way, only to find milliseconds later that a Dodge, with red light flashing, was in hot pursuit.

Coming down off the last rise on Sunset, Zack saw the ocean glistening before him. He was so hyped that he punched the accelerator even harder. The car leapt forward like a bullet exiting the muzzle of a forty-four magnum. Extreme G-force slammed Zack against the back of his seat. He was rocketing forward so fast that he never distinguished between the black and white squad cars that had stopped traffic at the intersection and the gawkers in the parking lot who were standing around trying to see what was going on. Yes, there was an opening for a car to make a turn, but no, physics hadn't yet devised a way for an automobile traveling in excess of a hundred miles an hour to make a sharp left. When Zack attempted to do so, the Porsche spun like a top and banged against the far curve, literally flipping it and sending it airborne. Its speed and centrifugal force were so great that it literally flew over the heads of diners at the outdoor tables. As the hysterical customers dove for cover on the boardwalk and under benches, the momentum of the catapulting car carried it airborne until gravity took over. The red racer landed initially on a row of jagged rocks that cracked it like a walnut and sent it tumbling toward the incoming tide. It bounced twice before coming to rest upside down with water lapping at what was left of the mostly crushed roof. The inversion was only momentary, however, as seconds later the mangled car burst into flames and black smoke began to rise into the sky irritating the hell out of a flock of screaming seagulls.

When the pursuing detectives eventually made their way through the gob-smacked crowd and looked out over the railing at what was left of the smoldering wreck, Russo couldn't help himself. He simply turned to Jamison and said, "Hooray for fucking Hollywood."

CHAPTER 20

ED NORMAN HAD JUST FINISHED a ham and cheese sandwich and washed it down with the dishwater that passed for coffee on his floor of the precinct. Eating at his desk was just about his least favorite thing to do but it was becoming more common as cases continued to pile up. The phone on his desk rang and he answered it.

"Detective Norman."

"Ed, this is Brig. I'm back at the hotel. Wanted to see if anything's come up on the Stanton killing."

"It's come up, all right. Up and over."

"What do you mean?"

"Sent two of my guys out to question Brady and Richards. Nothing special on the Brady front. You must not have turned on the TV in your room."

"I haven't. But what's that got to do with anything?"

"When my boys went over to have a chat with Richards, before they could even get a question in... the guy took off like a bat out of hell in some wicked-ass sports car. Russo and Jamison gave chase but the bastard hit Sunset and Highway One doing about a hundred. The car flipped, flew, crashed, and eventually wound up on the beach side of Gladstone's with Richards roasted to death in a burnt-out hulk. The press is having a field day with it."

"Jesus. Your guys never got to talk to him?"

"No. He blasted off the moment he made them as cops."

"Must have thought they were moving on him for the Stanton murder," Ellis said.

"That's my opinion," Norman replied. "Problem is we don't really have anything for sure. One of the crew members said he thought Richards may have been doing a little nose candy. Hell, for all we know he could have freaked out over anything and just decided to run like hell."

"Run from what?" Ellis asked again.

"Like I said, probably running from being connected to a murder. But *probably* isn't worth dick in a murder investigation."

"Think there was enough left of the body or the car for your forensic guys to come away with anything."

"Hard to say. Russo said it was definitely smoked."

"Damn, Ed. I talked to the guy a couple of days ago. He might have been high at the time. And he was more than pissed that we could expose what Dane had been holding over his head. But I never got a vibe that he was likely to hurt Iris Stanton in any way. What's the connection there? If he did kill her... why?"

"Maybe he thought, or knew, or thought he knew that Stanton had whatever Dane had. She had been the guy's personal assistant. Maybe he was afraid she'd blackmail him as well?"

"Ed, the missing drawer had potentially compromising material on her as well. Material she would have gotten rid of if she knew of its existence."

"You and I know that. Richards didn't. Anyway, one of the things I've learned about police work is that it's a dead end to keep trying to figure out what you don't know when you could be focusing on what you do know. So, as of now, what do we know?"

"We know Dane had something on five different people."

"You haven't brought me up to speed on what all that stuff is yet, you know."

"I do know, Ed, and I will, but for the moment let's think this out. The five people we're looking into were all in the hotel when he was killed. We're pretty positive he had something on each of them that they didn't want him to have. Two of those people are now dead. Someone tried to make it look like Iris Stanton committed suicide. Zack Richards may have been the one to do that, before killing himself in a car crash. But why kill Iris? And why try to make it look like she killed herself?"

"Brig, you just detoured right out of what we *think* we know into what we *don't*. So, let's keep working two fronts here. You stay focused on the Dane case, and I'll keep Russo and Jamison dogging the Stanton murder. That will make things a lot less complicated and hopefully get to a resolution quicker. Plus, now we've got two fewer suspects to worry about for the Dane killing."

"Wrong Ed. Just because they're dead, that doesn't necessarily mean one of them wasn't the person who killed Abel Dane."

"You got a point there, Brig. Getting yourself killed doesn't even get you scratched off a suspect list. Life's a bitch, ain't it?"

CHAPTER 21

BRADY THOUGHT YAMASHIRO'S SEEMED THE perfect place for a clandestine meeting. It was like hiding in plain sight. The Japanese restaurant situated two hundred and fifty feet high in the Hollywood hills offered a spectacular view of the city. It had been around since 1914. As such, it was the sort of place every tourist would seek out, but one would be hard-pressed to find any working members of the movie business there. However, if the trio was seen together, the screenwriter could always come up with an excuse as to why that particular threesome was sharing a table. Making up stories was his livelihood.

Jocelyn was the last to arrive. As she sat down she looked at Brady and said, "You were the one who said there'd be no reason for us ever to get together again."

Brady replied, "I believe it was the poet Robert Burns who said, '*The best laid schemes o' mice an' men / Gang aft agley*'."

Yuri quickly added, "And I think it was the boxer Mike Tyson who said, 'Everyone has a plan until you get hit in the mouth.'"

"Have we been hit in the mouth?" Jocelyn asked.

"It's certainly beginning to feel that way," Yuri answered.

"Look, both of you, there's no reason to panic. Apparently,

that's what Zack did and we see what that did to him. I wanted us to get together to make sure we're as aligned tonight as we were months ago."

"But what about poor Iris?" Jocelyn interjected. "Is her death connected in some way to Zack's?"

"It's impossible to know right now," Brady answered. "I assume the police didn't share any details about her death with either of you?"

"Not with me," Jocelyn quickly replied.

"Or me," Yuri added.

"The two who saw me didn't go into it either. They usually keep a lid on details to see if any suspects might mention something only the killer would know about."

Yuri jumped in. "You said *two* cops saw you? Only this Ellis fellow has spoken to me."

"Ellis was the one who came to my house as well," Jocelyn added.

"I had been interviewed by Ellis initially," Brady explained, "About Abel. But the two officers who came to see me, the ones looking into Iris's death, seemed to be unaware of any further investigation into the Dane case."

Yuri said, "I'll have another glass of that."

"And one for me." Jocelyn volunteered.

Sam had ordered a bottle of Saki for the table when he first arrived, telling the waiter that he'd signal him when his party was ready for menus. This would keep interruptions to a minimum, which it had so far. The three were about halfway through the bottle.

"I know I asked you this before," Jocelyn said, "but what do you really think, Sam? Do you think Zack had anything to do with Iris's death?"

"It's possible I guess. Zack knew the police were circling

back on Abel's death. He might have felt that Iris was the most vulnerable. The most honest perhaps. The one most likely to reveal something about the lottery to the police. Plus, my understanding is that he had been powdering his nose quite a bit lately."

"But look," Yuri interjected, "as terrible as Iris's and Zack's deaths are, it's not really about that, is it? It's about the fact that the police—particularly this Ellis fellow—know more about us than they should. At least he does about me. I assume it's the same with the two of you."

"Yes, he knows what Abel was holding over my head," Jocelyn replied.

"He thinks he may know about me," Sam said. "But the fact is… he's not in a position to prove anything. Not yet anyway. Even if he knows why we may have wanted Abel out of the way, he's got no clue regarding our actions, no way to get a clue unless one of us talks, and certainly no way to know who actually killed Abel. I mean we don't even know that, right?"

"Only the killer knows," Jocelyn said. "Your plan saw to that, Sam."

Yuri added, "So Abel's killer could already be dead. Or sitting at this table."

"That's always been the beauty of it," Sam replied. "In our silence, and our lack of knowledge, lies our safety. So what if Ellis has a motive for each of us? He has no proof who killed Abel, and no proof of conspiracy."

"Unless," Jocelyn said meekly, "Iris talked before she died."

"I don't think that's the case, Jocelyn," Sam responded. "If so, they would have hauled us all in by now."

"So we just keep quiet, then?" Yuri began. "We say nothing? We admit nothing?"

"Exactly," Sam confirmed. "And don't fall for any of those

police tricks. They may come to you and say that they know one of us did it, and the first one to talk gets the best deal. They may tell you that one of us has already spilled the beans, so you might as well confirm. Don't buy it. Stay strong. Get on with your lives. Lives we can all live now that Abel Dane isn't around to make us his damned puppets."

"I think I'll be going," Jocelyn said. "I'm not in the mood to eat."

"Well, it's probably better if we leave at separate times anyway," Sam responded. "Go ahead. Just remember, we're still in this together."

"I know. I know we are. Goodbye," Jocelyn said as she stood and walked quickly away.

"I'm not very hungry either, Sam."

"Well, stay for one more drink, just to stagger departures. And Yuri, I can count on your silence, right?"

"Absolutely."

"Good."

After he finished his drink, Yuri left, leaving Sam to tell the waiter he'd be the only one dining that night.

"I see," the waiter responded. Then asked, "You buy for one but tip for three?"

"In your dreams, Tojo," Sam replied. "I'm not from out of town."

CHAPTER 22

AFTER LEAVING YAMASHIRO'S, YURI COULDN'T shake the feeling that everything seemed to be coming apart. The thoughts careening around his brain matched the winding road he had to maneuver his Porsche over to make his way down the hill, past The Magic Castle, onto North Sycamore, and eventually left on Hollywood Boulevard. How and why was Iris killed? What prompted Zack to freak out? Could he trust Sam and Jocelyn to keep their secret? And it wasn't just them. That damned Ellis was onto the passport discrepancy. How long would it be before he, or maybe even other government officials came asking more questions about that? How did everything start to go so badly, particularly when so much time had passed since Abel's death?

With his mind crammed full, Yuri failed to notice the Ford sedan that had picked him up at the bottom of the hill and was following him into the city. The two men in the car didn't speak and kept their attention solely focused on the object of their assignment. They had been given leeway in how they were to carry out their objective, but the primary directive was precise. Make it look natural or like an accident initially. If sometime later it was exposed as being premeditated, that could be dealt with diplomatically. Time and obfuscation work wonders.

Having followed Yuri previously, to get a feel for his habits, the two had worked out a plan. So they kept a reasonable distance between their car and his. Even though traffic was heavy on Hollywood Boulevard, they weren't distracted by the stop-and-go that streetlights enforced, or the plethora of people on the sidewalks strolling between theaters, restaurants, tattoo parlors, and tourist traps. They had done their sightseeing already and now were all business. Showtime was approaching.

Near the Pantages Theater, Yuri turned north onto Vine. Once off the far more heralded street, both road and walkway traffic usually thinned out sharply. This evening was no exception. In fact, there appeared to be no one about. Across from the Capitol Records building, there was a bar that Yuri often stopped in for a nightcap before returning to his apartment. He felt the need for one now.

The duo following him had seen this behavior before. When Yuri pulled to the curb and parked on the opposite side of the street from his destination, behind a tricked-out Ram pickup truck, the Ford's driver killed his headlights and stopped about forty yards from their prey.

Yuri stepped out of his car slowly and stretched. When he did, the man behind the wheel of the Ford stomped the gas pedal to the floor. Yuri was in the process of locking his door when the sedan came barreling out of the darkness, sideswiped the Porsche, and smashed the Ukrainian filmmaker between his own car and the truck in front of him. Pinned there, his pelvis shattered and his back broken, he was immobile and still barely breathing. The Ford came to a full stop just past the carnage. The man on the passenger side hurriedly exited and ran back to check on their handiwork. When he saw that Yuri wasn't dead yet, the man looked him in the eye and with a heavy Russian accent said, "Ukrainian filth. Revolutionary, huh? Vladimir Putin does not forget." Then he grabbed Yuri by the head, and jerked it violently to one side snapping the spinal cord." Death was instantaneous.

The man quickly returned to the Ford and the two were swallowed by the night before patrons started to scramble out of the bar wondering what the noise had been. Seeing the dreadful aftermath, one onlooker could only gasp, "My God, it must have been a hit-and-run."

CHAPTER 23

NEWSPAPER REPORTS THE FOLLOWING DAY referred to a traffic accident on Vine resulting in the death of Yuri Kaminski, an up-and-coming film director. Ellis ran across the article as he scanned the *L.A. Times* digital edition on his computer. He was quickly on the phone to Ed Norman after he saw it. Norman suggested that perhaps it was time for a sit down between himself, Ellis, and the two officers pursuing the Stanton murder. "I don't necessarily think four heads are better than one," Norman said, "but there's just too much going down too quickly. We need to get on top of this."

An interview room at the police station served as the locale for the meet. Norman and Ellis were already seated at a metal table when Russo and Jamison joined them. After introductions, handshakes, and explanations by Norman of who was doing what and why, they got down to the business of give and take.

"Okay, a quick recap," Norman began. "We had five people we were looking at for the Dane murder. Three of the five are now dead. Iris Stanton killed, and whoever did it attempted to make it look like suicide. Zack Richards killed, running from having to explain himself to the police. Yuri Kaminski killed in some weird hit-and-run. Bodies are dropping like falling dominoes, gentleman. We need to start putting some pieces together. Are these deaths related to one another? And are they all tied to the Dane murder?"

Russo jumped in first. "Well, it seems obvious that Richards had something to do with the Stanton murder or he wouldn't have taken off like that?"

Jamison chimed in, "Of course, there were reports that he was high as a kite that morning and coke heads are known to do some weird things for little or no reason."

"No one has yet been able to tie Richards directly to the Stanton murder," Norman added. "While he may have done a piss-poor job of making it look like a suicide... if he did it... he did a great job of cleaning up after himself. No prints anywhere. And... what about motive?"

Russo came back. "So we have a lady dead and we don't know why. We have one guy who couldn't handle the car he was driving, and he's dead, but we're not sure why? Then we have this other guy, this Kaminski, who appears to have been killed in a hit-and-run, which could have been an accident or could have been premeditated. And as I said before, we don't know why?"

"So, what the hell do we know?" Jamison asked.

"I can speak to that," Ellis interjected. "We know the five suspects in the Dane murder all had possible motives. And while each motive was different, apparently they were all being manipulated by Dane to do his bidding."

Norman said, "Fill them in, Brig."

"Based on what I found, here's what I think. Dane may have known that Sam Brady didn't actually write the screenplay for the movie that won him an Oscar. If that were the case, he could have gotten Brady thrown out of the business. Dane had what appeared to be compromising photos of Iris Stanton, but she didn't know that until long after he was dead. So, other than potential workplace harassment, her motive's a bit fuzzy. Richards had been in some low-rent kiddie-porn that Dane had a tape of. Dane must have been holding it over his head. But that doesn't tell us anything about why Richards would want Iris Stanton dead."

When no one ventured an answer, Ellis kept going.

"It looks like Kaminski may have been allowed to enter the U. S. and work here illegally. Dane apparently had the goods on who he really was. So Kaminski would have to adhere to whatever Dane wanted. As for the fifth suspect, Jocelyn Hayward, she had a potential motive, too."

"Which is?" Norman asked.

"For now, Ed, let's just say it's sex-related. I told her I'd keep a lid on it unless and until I had to divulge it in detail, in which case I'd let her know in advance."

"Making deals with suspects is not part of our standard operating procedure," Norman said. "But you can sit on it for the moment, Brig. Until it becomes need-to-know. The point is… she too had a potential motive for icing Dane, right?"

"Right."

"Let me get this straight," Russo cut in. "While we like Richards for the murder of Stanton, we don't have motive or evidence to pin it on him. And when it comes to this Dane guy, you've got five different people with five different motives, but no evidence on any of them?"

"Sound's like shit's creek to me," Jamison volunteered.

Before any of the others could respond, a young woman in uniform came into the room without knocking and handed a set of papers to Ed Norman.

"This just came in," she said.

"Thanks," Norman responded. Then after quickly perusing what he had been given, Norman said, "Hmm. The plot thickens."

Russo asked, "How so, chief?"

"Looks like it was a rental car that did the damage to Kaminski. Car was turned in with passenger-side damage. The blood found on it matched Kaminski's DNA."

"Who rented it?" Ellis asked.

"Two zombies apparently," Norman replied. "Needless to say they didn't stick around when they returned the car. Just left it in the parking lot. When the rental company back-checked the ID info that was used to rent the car initially, it turned out to be bogus. The name, numbers, addresses, and everything were for some guy who died a couple of years ago in Illinois."

"Identity theft," Russo surmised.

"Yep," Norman confirmed.

Jamison asked, "Do they have visual descriptions or anything at all on whoever rented the car?"

Norman continued reading the message. "Still have a copy of the fake ID. And the clerk who handled the rental remembered that the guy spoke with a heavy accent. Thinks it might have been Russian."

"Russian?" Ellis said, to no one in particular. "And Kaminski was Ukrainian. Not much difference in those accents to the untrained ear. Maybe the guy was Ukrainian, too."

"Whatever he is, he's probably long gone." Russo said.

"Back to the motherland, I bet," Norman added. "What do you think, Brig? Connection, red herring, or wild-ass coincidence?"

"Two out of three, maybe. These days there's no love lost between the Ruskies and the Ukrainians. And it's a pretty solid bet Kaminski was here on a fake passport. If Dane found out about that, maybe we can too. Any chance of backtracking on it?"

"Yep. It'll take a while. But we'll get the ball rolling," Norman replied.

"Something you said a minute ago," Russo started.

"Me?" Norman asked.

"No, Ellis."

"What did I say?"

"You said, that all five of the Dane suspects were being manipulated to do his bidding."

"Yes. That's what it looks like.

"Okay," Russo began, "what if… just for the sake of argument… we assume for a minute… that they all did it."

"What's that supposed to mean?" Norman asked.

"Did you ever see that old movie" Russo replied, "*Murder on the Orient Express?* It's about this murder on a train. And it turns out there were a whole bunch of people… I forget exactly how many… but they were all in cahoots with one another and each of them took turns stabbing this guy who was already asleep. So they all did it. Even though the poor dude was probably long dead before the last few stabbed him. What do you think? Is that possible with this Dane thing?"

"That kind of shit happens in the movies," Jamison volunteered. "Not in real life."

"If you haven't noticed," Russo retorted, "these are movie people we're talking about."

Norman interjected. "There were three shots—not five—fired in rapid order in the Dane killing. There's no way five people could have been in the hallway, shot the guy, and gotten back to their individual rooms without causing a lot more stir than was caused."

"But," Ellis ventured, "Maybe there's something to what Detective Russo suggested. "What if it wasn't all five? What if it was just one, but the other four knew about it?"

"Come on," Norman said, "who kills somebody and goes out of his or her way to have four other people know about it?"

"Yeah," Jamison added, "that's like getting out of Dutch with one person to be at the mercy of four others. Nobody would do that."

"Hey," Russo piped up. "I was just spitballing. It's not like we've got a lot of alternative assumptions to evaluate, you know."

"So, where do we go from here?" Jamison asked.

Norman took over. "Based on the info we got a minute ago, let's assume the Kaminski hit-and-run was pre-planned. A hit by someone, or some government, or both, who wanted him dead for something that happened in Europe before he got here. His illegal efforts to gain entry with a potentially forged passport point to that being the case. If it is, the Kaminski killing is more of an outlier to what we've been talking about. Now, how about the Stanton murder?"

"Still like Richards for that," Russo volunteered. "He acted like a killer on the run."

"Yes, but what about motive?" Norman asked.

"You know," Ellis began hesitantly, "if there is anything to what Russo was suggesting about some sort of conspiracy, well, perhaps Richards thought that Iris was the weakest link in the chain. The one most likely to break and talk about what went on. If he believed that, he would have felt at risk, too. Maybe so at risk that he was compelled to eliminate her and try to make it look like she killed herself because she couldn't deal with a new investigation."

Russo came back into the conversation. "Which also means,

if he killed her for the reason you say, then it's unlikely she was Dane's killer, and more likely it was Richards."

"That seems more likely," Ellis responded. "Of course, it's also possible that Kaminski or Brady killed her, too. Or, that Richards killed her for some reason we know nothing about."

"If we believe that," Norman cut in, "then we have to believe the Stanton killing had nothing to do with the Dane murder. And if it didn't, that means we have not one, but two murders, Stanton and Kaminski, plus one accidental death, Richards, that have nothing whatsoever to do with the murder of Abel Dane. And fellas… that I am *not* buying."

"So, back to the question I asked a minute ago," Jamison said. "Where do we go from here?"

Norman answered. "Nutty or not, let's assume there might be something in what Russo was suggesting. Some kind of potential conspiracy. There are only two of the five conspirators left. One of which might be a killer… one or both might be conspirators but not the actual triggerman… and like it or not… it's still possible that neither of them are killers or conspirators and that both Dane's and Stanton's killer may already be dead."

Russo asked, "You want us to help out on this Dane thing, Ed?"

"My sainted mother used to say too many cooks spoil the broth. So, no. I want you and Jamison to dig deeper into the Stanton murder. Go back over anything and everything that Richards may have left behind at his home, the studio where he worked, whatever. Get a court order if you have to."

"Will do, boss."

"Brig, you circle back with Jocelyn Hayward and see what you can do to shed more light on this whole thing. Push her as hard as you need to. And dial up the pressure on Sam Brady too. We need to get to the bottom of this goddamned morass. I'm tired of bodies piling up while we have no idea who's doing the piling."

CHAPTER 24

ELLIS DECIDED THE BEST WAY to deal with Sam Brady was to surprise him. So rather than set up a call, he noted the writer's home address in the file and drove to his bungalow in Santa Monica. Ringing the doorbell produced no results. Neither did rapping on the door with his knuckles. Shouting the man's name and hoping for a response ended in failure also. So Ellis rationalized that if needed, he could always cop to entering because he was in the heat of a murder investigation. Sounds plausible, Ellis thought, as he removed the same lock-picking tool that he had used to get into Iris Stanton's apartment. It worked on Brady's door as well. Stepping in, he spoke loudly. "Hello. Is anyone home? Brady? Sam Brady, are you here? This is police business. Hello?"

No response. Ellis began to wander through the bungalow looking for nothing in particular, but being careful to leave no signs that he had been there at all. As he was getting ready to leave, he noticed an answering machine on a side table. There was no blinking light indicating waiting messages, so Ellis pulled his cell phone out and rang Brady's number.

The recording said: "Brady here. Out of town for a couple of days. Leave your name and number. I'll get back to you first thing Thursday morning."

That means he's getting back to L.A. sometime tonight, Ellis said to himself. Of course, it could be early or it could be late. Oh well, cross that bridge later.

Since it was still morning, he decided to drive to Jocelyn Hayward's house. However, the faster he drove and the closer he got to the actress's home, the more he realized that a change in tactics was definitely in order. Jocelyn had been adamant when she and Ellis met before—no more discussions regarding the Dane murder without her attorney present. Understandable, Ellis thought. Especially once he had proffered the hypothetical that Dane was her child's father. But Ellis hoped he wouldn't have to go through a formal meeting with Jocelyn and her defense attorney—with him on one side of an interrogation table and them on the other. Rather, he hoped for an encounter where she wouldn't have professional backup. To improve the likelihood of that, he didn't let her know he was coming and parked just down the street from her house. Before he could walk from his car to her gate, however, the garage door opened and a convertible Mercedes 350 exited the subterranean garage with Jocelyn behind the wheel. Having been with her a day earlier, he was sure it was her, even though there had been a minimal attempt at camouflage. A colorful Hermes scarf was wrapped tightly around her head, shrouding completely her raven black hair. Sunshades with lenses just slightly smaller than sunflowers covered her eyes and most of the middle of her face. She would still be gawked at by drivers or pedestrians passing by, but the two elements of her disguise would probably need to be removed for anyone to recognize her immediately.

Ellis quickly returned to his car and keeping his distance, followed as she wound her way toward Beverly Hills. Towering palm trees and stately mansions bordered both sides of the streets she traversed until she turned onto Wilshire Boulevard. Then she stayed in the right-hand lane until she took a right turn onto Avenue of the Stars. From there it was only moments before she drove into the entrance of The Century City Hotel. Ellis slowed down just enough so she had time to leave her car with an attendant, before walking toward the lobby. He then swung in quickly before the attendant had time to get in her vehicle and take it away. Parking directly behind her new Mercedes with his classic one, he hailed the young man and said, "I'm with the lady that just arrived, have to hurry to catch her."

The attendant, realizing the value of treating customers well, quickly tore another ticket off his pad and handed it to Ellis who accepted it with one hand and passed a twenty-dollar bill to the young man with his other. "Keep it close, will you? Not sure how long I'm going to be"

"Certainly, sir. Will do."

Scanning the lobby as he walked in, Ellis saw Jocelyn in conversation with a female clerk behind the check-in desk. The clerk reached under the counter, pulled out a package, and hesitated before handing it to Jocelyn. Ellis assumed the employee needed to be sure she was giving the right thing to the right person. Jocelyn took her wallet out of her purse and had the girl look at it. The clerk nodded, smiled, and handed the package over. Then the actress walked over to a secluded nook in the corner of the lobby and took a seat in one of two plush chairs separated only by a small round table. As she was opening the package and pulling its contents out, Ellis stepped over and took a seat in the other chair.

Jocelyn glanced at him quickly, looked down at the script she had just taken from the package, and tried to decide whether to adopt an attitude or not. For his part, Ellis had already made up his mind to try a bit of subterfuge. She had probably already heard about Kaminski's death, but there was no way she could know who was really behind it. Perhaps he could use that to his advantage.

"Mr. Ellis, I thought I made myself clear when we last met—"

"There's been a new development."

"I'm just here to pick up this script that was left for me and I have to—"

"You must have seen or heard about Kaminski's death."

"It's so dreadful. A hit-and-run. How could someone not stop to help."

"Help wasn't on the agenda."

"What do you mean?"

"I mean the hit-and-run wasn't an accident. It was simply meant to look like one."

"But who would do such a thing?"

"Perhaps someone who is tying up loose ends."

"I'm sorry, I don't really follow you."

"Let me give you directions. Let's say there was more than one person who had it in for Abel Dane as much as you did. Maybe a group of people. Let's say those individuals got together and decided to do something about it. Which, by the way, is called conspiracy to commit murder. And that's a crime that carries with it a lot of jail time. Anyway... the deed gets done. Abel Dane gets killed. Now let's say the person who did the actual killing thinks he's gotten away with it because months go by and the investigation goes cold. But then something causes it to heat up again. The killer knows there are other people who can finger him as the one who did it. He gets scared. He gets paranoid. He decides to eliminate anyone who can tie him to the murder. Iris Stanton is killed. Zack Richards dies. Yuri Kaminski is knocked off. Personally, if I happened to be part of that rogue's gallery, I'd be getting extremely nervous right now."

Jocelyn tried to counter. "But Zack Richards wasn't murdered. The news said he died in a car accident."

"He did. The killer got something for nothing there. That doesn't necessarily change the rest of his plan."

By now, Jocelyn had put the script down on the table and was massaging both temples with her hands. She was troubled about the recent deaths of her co-conspirators. She was concerned about what Ellis already knew about her and Dane. "Mr. Ellis, you told me that you wouldn't reveal my connection to Abel Dane without telling me first."

"Yes. And I haven't. But frankly, it looks like I may have to. More importantly, don't you realize that you're in danger too? You could be the next loose end that gets tied."

Jocelyn's thoughts raced back to her meeting at Yamashiro's. Brady said the police would try something like this. Pitting one person against another. But Kaminski was alive then. Now he isn't. Could Brady actually be killing the other conspirators? The whole plan was his idea, devised precisely to keep the murderer's identity secret. Maybe *he* was melting down. And if he was, she could wind up like Iris and Kaminski, and her son could wind up an orphan.

Jocelyn then did an odd thing. She reached over and put her hand just under Ellis's throat. Then she ran her fingertips slowly down the middle of his chest until they reached his waist. "You aren't wearing one of those wires, are you? Recording what we say. In the movies, someone is always wearing one."

"No. I'm not wearing a wire. This conversation is just

between you and me."

"So, if I were to tell you something, I mean anything really, and then recanted later... well, it would just be my word against yours, right?"

"That's right. Do you have something you want to tell me?"

"I want to, but I'm afraid. Afraid for myself and my son."

"You're in a lot more danger than your son at the moment. But if you share something with me that leads to finding Dane's killer, then the police can protect both you and him."

"And afterward, what about that? If I was involved in what you called a conspiracy, would I have to go to jail?"

"Hard to say. You'd definitely get credit for helping catch a murderer. And with a high-priced celebrity lawyer at your side—that I'm sure you can afford—I wouldn't be surprised if you wound up with some sort of probation or maybe even a suspended sentence out of the whole thing. But I can't promise that."

For the first time, Jocelyn removed her sunglasses and looked Ellis directly in the eye.

"And I can't promise I won't deny everything we're about to discuss if it looks like something's going terribly wrong. Remember Mr. Ellis, I'm an excellent actress."

CHAPTER 25

THE PHONE ON ED NORMAN'S desk rang. He reached over and took the receiver from the cradle without looking up from the paperwork he was going over.

"This is Detective Norman."

"Ed, it's me Brig. Hope you're sitting down."

"Well, I am, but why?"

"I didn't want you to fall over when you hear what I've got. Oh, and you might want to consider giving Russo a raise."

"Enough with the setup. What do you have?"

"It's going to cost something, Ed. You'll have to look into some sort of deal with the District Attorney or you won't get the testimony. She'll deny our conversation ever took place."

"Which 'she' and what conversation... and what the hell was that about Russo?"

"The 'she' is Jocelyn Hayward. The conversation is what we need to wrap this thing up. And Russo's idea about more than one person being involved is the key."

"Look, Brig. Just take it from the top and tell me exactly what you have."

"According to Jocelyn Hayward, all five of the people we've been looking into were involved in a plot to bump Dane off. It was all put together by Sam Brady. He had this idea about a lottery. You know, like drawing straws. Whoever got the short straw had to kill Dane. Except, no straws were involved. Numbers were put in a hat and each person had to draw. Whoever drew the number one had to do the deed. But no one was allowed to see each other's number. So four of the five people would know they didn't do it, but they'd have no idea who did the actual killing."

"How'd you get this out of her," Norman asked.

"I suggested that we knew there was some sort of conspiracy, but we didn't know the details. I also indicated that Kaminski's death was part of a pattern. And the pattern was Dane's real killer was doing away with anyone who could connect him to the murder."

"But we know Kaminski was killed by the Russians."

"We know that. She didn't. And when she realized that Brady could be taking the others out, she came across with what I've told you."

"You believe her?"

"I do."

"You never told me what her beef with Dane was."

"Here's what I was holding back, and we need to keep a lid on it if we can. If it gets out too loud or too soon, she may not cooperate. Dane in essence raped her. She got pregnant and refused to abort. He paid for everything, hospital, birth, and putting the child in a Catholic home. But he forced her to give him legal claim to the child and if she ever exposed him as the father, she'd lose any parenting rights she might have later. He was keeping her away from the kid unless she'd make his films."

"Wow. What a swell, guy. But how do we know for certain that Brady killed Dane?"

"Just seems to make sense, Ed. Brady's a writer. He could

come up with a plan like that. In fact, he could have even fixed it so that Dane would wind up dead, regardless."

"What do you mean fixed it? And regardless of what?"

"Think about it. He's got four people who hate Dane like he does. But they're just people, not stone-cold assassins. Suppose whoever draws that number one... chickens out, and doesn't go through with it. He winds up with Dane still running his life, and now he's got four people who could make it even worse."

"So... how does he fix it?"

"He puts five numbers in the hat. Everyone has to draw a number. Whoever draws number one has to kill Dane. But there is no number one. He doesn't put it in. He puts in one of the other numbers twice. No one's allowed to let anyone see what number each person drew, so no one knows who the real killer is. Brady makes sure that Dane is killed because he does it himself. And there's no way the others can know for sure it was him."

"Jesus. What a crafty bastard."

"Now the 'fixing it' angle is conjecture on my part, Ed. But the rest comes straight out of Jocelyn Hayward's mouth."

"And you think she'll testify."

"Depends on the deal, and whether she'll still be in a position to be granted legal custody of her son."

"Well, the D. A.'s been known to do some wheeling and dealing in his time. And it would be a feather in his cap to be able to put a high-profile cold case like the Dane murder away."

"Hey, I almost forgot," Ellis interjected. "I found out Brady's been out of town but he'll be back sometime tonight. Should we be waiting for him?"

Norman paused momentarily, then said, "Better wait.

Let me run this whole thing by the D. A. first. No point in grabbing him if we don't know whether the D. A.'s office is willing to deal. And if Brady's coming back to town, then he doesn't appear to be running. Just hold off until I tell you it's a go."

"Okay. But if you don't mind, I might pull my own watch for a bit on Jocelyn Hayward. It's not out of the realm of possibility that Brady might want to eliminate anyone who's left that could finger him."

"Makes sense. Go ahead and keep an eye on her. And by the way, thanks. You remember when you asked me why I wanted you involved? I said you had a way of getting people to open up, to share things they might not share with somebody else. Guess I was right about that, huh?"

"Well, this time anyway. Just wish I had been able to turn something up sooner. Then we might not have lost Iris Stanton."

"That one's not on you, Brig. Fortunes of war."

"Make that *mis*fortunes."

CHAPTER 26

SAM BRADY GOT BACK TO his Santa Monica bungalow just after eleven p.m. The short return flight from San Francisco wasn't what fatigued him, his tiredness was due to the long hours he had spent in story conferences over the last couple of days regarding a cop show that was being developed called City by the Bay. Sam wanted to write it. The producers weren't sure they wanted him. The meetings had been exhausting. Even though he was wasted, he couldn't keep himself from scrolling through his laptop one last time before going to bed. After emails, he checked the local news, where he found a short paragraph with a long headline reading: HOLLYWOOD DIRECTOR KILLED IN HIT-AND-RUN ACCIDENT.

Finding Yuri Kaminski's name in the first paragraph was a shock. *My God*, he said to himself, *we just got together a few days ago*. Brady was about to pick up the phone and call Jocelyn Hayward, but the late hour made him think twice. Embedded in that second thought was the realization that he didn't really know what he'd say to her. Their little group was just down to Jocelyn and him now. Would the police push harder and try to pit one against the other? He remembered telling the actress and Kaminski that they probably would.

But he was just too bushed to pursue it immediately. He decided to talk to her tomorrow.

Brady rose the following morning, showered, shaved, and left his condo on foot. He was on his way to Amelia's for his bi-monthly breakfast with friends from the Writers Guild. The morning was clear and cool and he looked at the cloudless blue sky frequently as he strolled along the sidewalk. There was no reason for him to pay any attention to the car that had been following him since he left his bungalow. It kept its distance by creeping, stopping, and starting again to maintain separation. Still a few blocks from his destination, Brady realized he had failed to bring his cigarettes with him. There was a small bodega just a few yards in front of him though, so when he reached the front door, he stepped inside to pick up a pack of smokes. The driver of the car that had been following, jammed the accelerator down and raced ahead until it was parallel to the bodega's door. There he squealed to a stop, quickly pulled on a ski mask, flung open the car door, and raced inside with gun in hand.

"Give me all the money in the register!" he shouted to the clerk. "And nobody make a move!" Brady and an older woman frozen in fear by the refrigerated beverages were the only customers in the store. The clerk dropped Brady's pack of cigarettes on the counter. When he turned to the register to get the cash, Brady, without thinking, reached out to retrieve his smokes. "No moves," barely got out of the robber's mouth before his gun went off and a single bullet went into Sam Brady's head. The woman screamed as Brady's body collapsed in a heap. The clerk froze with the cash in his hand. The bandit swiped the bills and darted for the door. In his haste, he used his hand holding the gun to push it open. But when he did, his momentum knocked the weapon from his hand and the gun fell to the floor causing another round to discharge. The woman screamed again. The clerk began reaching for something beneath the counter. The robber never stopped. He flung himself through the entrance, across the sidewalk, and into his car. Then burning rubber, he squealed away from the curb and down the street.

It had all happened in less than a minute. The woman was leaning against the cooler door with her hand pressed against her heart. The clerk was on the cell phone he had been reaching for to call 911. And Sam Brady was lying dead on the floor clutching a pack of Camels.

CHAPTER 27

ELLIS HAD JUST GOTTEN BACK to his hotel room from his morning jog. He was sweating profusely and about to jump in the shower when his cell phone rang.

"This is Brig Ellis."

"Brig, Ed.

"Hey, Ed. So how did it go with the District Attorney?"

"It didn't. I haven't spoken to him. Something else has come up."

"Oh yeah, what's that?"

"Sam Brady is dead."

"What?"

"Yep. Happened this morning."

"But how... I mean what actually happened?"

"Apparently it was a case of wrong place, wrong time. A bodega got knocked off in Santa Monica. Brady was one of two customers inside. Looks like the perp panicked and shot him."

"What about the other customer?"

"A woman. She's okay. So is the store clerk."

"Maybe I should get over there and talk to them."

"Russo and Jamison are there already. They're getting all the info, but their initial take is a stick-up gone bad."

"Man. It's just hard to believe. I mean it looks like everyone involved with the Dane killing in any way is absolutely snake bit."

"Poisonous-ass snake, that's for sure."

"Russo got anything yet on the perp?"

"Nothing firm. Dude was wearing a ski mask to cover his face, plus heavy sweat clothes. Neither the other customer nor the clerk got a look at the getaway car."

"Did the customer and the clerk's statement match?"

"Come on, Brig, you know that's seldom the case. But Russo's working on it. We'll know more when he files a report."

"Jesus, Ed. So what about the Jocelyn Hayward thing? I mean we were pressing her to give up Brady. Now Brady's dead. Which means there's no threat to her from him. Plus there's no reason to involve herself and admit she told me about the whole lottery thing?"

"Good point. And we can't keep a lid on Brady's death. I'm sure by this afternoon there'll be all sorts of TV, radio, and Internet stories about an Oscar-winning writer being killed in a botched armed robbery."

"So what next?"

"Let me get Russo's report. It will be a lot more detailed. After I have that, we can really sort things out."

"Okay. Call me when you get it."

"Will do, Brig. And hey, why don't you take the rest of the day off? You've certainly earned it."

"I'm going to give that suggestion some serious thought, my friend. Talk to you later."

But after Ellis hung up, the thought of relaxation couldn't get past the thought that everyone involved in the Dane conspiracy was turning up dead—and there was only one conspirator left.

CHAPTER 28

JOCELYN HAYWARD SAW THE STORY about the robbery and shooting in Santa Monica on the midday news. By then, officials had released the name of the customer who was shot and killed. When Sam Brady's picture came up, the reporter referred to him as "former Oscar-winning screenwriter, Samuel Brady." Jocelyn gasped. Brady dead? How could it be? A robbery gone bad, they said. One person killed. But how could it have been Sam? It was both too awful and too... fortunate? What had Ellis intimated about Brady trying to tie up loose ends? Iris was dead. Zack too. Kaminski killed. Now Brady dead. Was it divine intervention? Whatever it was, Jocelyn now realized she wasn't just along for the ride, she was in the driver's seat. She didn't have to keep her agreement with Ellis. She didn't even have to admit there was any sort of conspiracy at all, or that the conversation with Ellis ever took place. Why take the chance of getting involved with an overly zealous, or worse still, an overly ambitious prosecutor? Why indeed?

It was mid-afternoon and Ellis had yet to hear from Norman. With nothing pressing on his agenda, he decided to go ahead and swing by the station to see if he could catch him there.

Traffic was light—if it can ever be called that in Los Angeles—and it didn't take him long to arrive. After checking in with the desk sergeant, he walked back to Norman's office. Nobody home. Stepping out into the squad room he saw Russo at his desk.

"Officer Russo, got a minute?"

"Oh, hey Ellis. What's happening?"

"I was just swinging by to see Ed, but he's not in his office."

"Yeah, I think he's involved in some personnel matter down the hall. Sometimes those meetings go on longer than planned"

"He said he was going to bring me up to speed on the Sam Brady killing after getting your report. If you've already turned it in, can I get the high points?"

"Sure, no problem. The thing has all the appearances of a bungled heist. Perp left his car running just outside, then ran in waving a piece and saying he wanted all the cash. Before the clerk could open the register and close the deal, Brady apparently made some sort of move and the idiot popped a cap in him. Then he grabbed the cash from the clerk and took off. Sucker was in such a hurry to get out of there that he knocked his gun out of his own hand trying to get the front door open. Didn't pause to pick it up. Just jumped in the car and hightailed it like a Nascar driver on his last lap."

"So you've got the gun that killed him. Anything on it yet?"

"Not initially. Beretta, .32 caliber. No prints. Plus the serial number was filed off. The boys in ballistics have it now. They'll get back to us, but with no number, it will be almost impossible to trace."

"Got a good description of the perp?"

"No. He had on a ski mask and sweats. No obvious accent.

In other words, he didn't sound black, Latin, or otherwise. But you never know. Still could be."

"How about the car?"

"A dark sedan. That's the most we got out of the clerk or the customer. Guess you can't blame 'em though. They'd just seen a guy get blown away. Had to be wondering at that moment if they were next. Plus, so many damn cars look alike today. Hard to tell one from another anyway."

"What time did you say it went down?"

"Just a little after eight according to the clerk."

"How long did it take for the call to come in and for Ed to send you over?"

"Call got routed through the 911 system. We heard from the Santa Monica boys about eight-thirty. They must have done a computer search and turned up Brady's name on the witness list in the Dane case. When they called and gave us the name of the deceased, we told them we'd be right there."

"You say they called *you*. Wonder why not Ed or me?"

"Ed wasn't in yet. He came in late this morning. Not sure about you. Have you downloaded any of your reports yet? I had one in there from our first interview with Brady about the Iris Stanton killing. That may have been where they got my name from."

"Yeah, probably so. I've been a bit lax in writing things up."

"Don't worry about it," Russo said. "This one's been a bit of a rat fuck from the get-go."

"What do you mean?"

"Well, you know. Me and Jamison covering one murder and you working a cold case that's related to it. No integration. No coordination. Hell, we didn't even know anything about your involvement until Ed got us all together the other day. Seems like a funny way to run a railroad."

"That's not the way it's usually done?"

"Nope. But hey, Ed's management, I'm labor, it's not for me to say."

Ellis responded. "Well, remember his comment the other day about 'too many cooks spoiling the broth.' Guess he really meant it."

"Never question a man who quotes his mother... especially if he's your boss."

"So, you think this meeting that Ed's in is going to break up anytime soon."

"No idea. Not the slightest."

"Well, if you're here when it does, tell him I came by, okay? He said he wanted to get together tonight. He can just give me a call and we can meet somewhere."

"I'll do that," Russo said. "And if I have to take off before it ends, I'll leave a note on his desk."

"Thanks. Appreciate it. Hope you find the dude that got Brady."

"Hope you turn up whoever iced Dane."

"Maybe we'll both get lucky,"

Going back to his paperwork, Russo responded, "I wouldn't count on it."

CHAPTER 29

ELLIS RETURNED TO HIS HOTEL for a quick swim, about a half hour lying in the sun by the pool, then back to his room for a shower. He tried to put the events of the last few days in some sort of new order, but they still came out in the same old place. Iris's murder made to look like suicide. Zack killed in a car crash, running away. Kaminski hit-and-run, probably on purpose. Now, Brady killed in a botched holdup. It was the last one that was gnawing at him. Just seemed way too conveniently random. Who would benefit from Brady's death? Jocelyn appeared to be the only one. No one to tie her to the lottery now. No one to hold anything over her head. But the witnesses said it was a guy. Of course, she could have paid to have it done. But what would be the point of getting rid of the last man that could tie her to a crime by hiring someone who could then tie her to a new crime? Made no sense. And was he any closer to knowing who killed Abel Dane? It definitely looked like Sam Brady orchestrated the whole thing, but did he actually pull the trigger? Probably, but still unknown.

Ed Norman had called when Brig was in the shower. He left a message suggesting they get together for dinner at Dan Tana's on Santa Monica Boulevard at eight o'clock. The restaurant in the little yellow house had been a fixture in West Hollywood since the mid-1960s. It had withstood the test of time with great food, service, and understated ambience that more than drew its share of celebrities. Yet Tana's treated every customer like every other one regardless of fame, fortune, or social status—another reason it had been around for over fifty years.

When Ellis arrived, Norman was already at the bar about to take his first sip of Woodford Reserve. The stool next to him was empty so Ellis took it.

"How many am I behind?"

"Just in time for the first," Norman said. "What'll it be?"

"What are you having?"

"Bourbon?"

"Count me in."

"And one for my friend," Norman told the barkeep.

When Ellis had his glass, Norman held his own up and said, "Here's to Happy Endings."

They clinked glasses and each took a drink. "Is that what we have here?" Ellis asked.

"Perhaps too soon to tell, my friend. Just seemed like a good thing to toast to."

"Indeed."

"Sorry I missed you at the station today. Russo told me you came by. I was up to my armpits in personnel crap. Damned shame, isn't it?"

"What's that?"

"The shit we have to wade through to get things done. We thought it was deep when we were in the service. But, man, I tell you. That was nothing compared to the city constabulary. Everybody, plus their associate assistant undersecretary of whatever, has an opinion about something, a directive that has to be followed, or a form that has to be filled out in triplicate and signed by every swinging dick who has a pay grade higher than mine—which is just about every swinging dick there is."

"Sounds like it was a hell of a meeting."

"I don't want to talk about it."

"Don't blame you. I've got the next round," Ellis said.

"Glad to hear it."

"Bartender... two more please."

It went that way for one additional round before the two decided to take their seats at one of the tufted leather booths. A bright red and white checked tablecloth added a feeling of hominess as they decided to slow down a bit and move from harder spirits to wine.

Norman began. "How about a bottle of Jordon Cabernet? This one's going to be on the city anyway, and hell, I mean we're going to eat meat, right?"

"We're men, aren't we?" Ellis asked rhetorically.

"Waiter, a bottle of Jordon Cabernet. Then we'll decide on dinner."

"Very good sir," the waiter replied, and left to fill the request.

After the arrival of the wine and halfway into their meal, Norman continued to bemoan the mountains of red tape required to get the smallest thing done on anything pertaining to personnel. Ellis watched and listened as his friend's frustration level rose and fell with the amount of vino in his glass. Eventually, they looped back around to the reason they were there in the first place.

"So Ed, with this latest development—"

"Which development is that?"

"Brady getting bumped off."

"Oh, yeah. What about it?"

"Well, I mean how do you want to proceed with Jocelyn Hayward?"

"Don't see how we can proceed."

"What do you mean?"

"I mean she'd have to be pretty damn loony to talk to law enforcement about her involvement now that no one can prove she was involved."

"Think she'd lie about what she told me?"

"Wouldn't you?"

"Think she'd say she never knew anything about any conspiracy and she was never involved in any way?"

"Wouldn't you?"

"Think she could live with herself knowing she had been right in the middle of those things?"

"She did a damn good job of it until this past week, didn't she? I mean we never heard a peep out of any of those people until you found a motive for all of them."

"Well, you're right about that."

"Brig," Norman began, pushing his plate away, leaning back, and crossing his legs, "you did what I brought you here to do. You found motives my guys couldn't. You even got a confession out of one of the bunch. My guys never got close to anything like that. If Brady hadn't been iced, we would have been ready to close the book once and for all on the killing of Abel Dane. Brady's initial idea, Brady's plan for the lottery, Brady fixing it, like you suggested, so he'd be the one to do the shooting and no one else could finger him. Looks to me like we're still ready to close that book."

"You're probably right. That's very likely what happened. But when you sent Russo and Jamison out to cover it, you must have found it pretty weird that the guy who planned it all got his ticket punched before we could pin it on him."

"I did. But I've learned to live with weird. Cops do it every day."

"Well, just for conversation's sake, let me lob one more softball out there."

"Lob away."

"What if the Brady killing wasn't random? What if Jocelyn Hayward paid to have someone kill Brady and make it appear to go down like it did."

"You don't really believe that."

"No. I don't, but we've each got a little wine left, so convince me that's impossible."

"Hey, in this crazy world, anything's possible. But here's why it's utterly improbable. One, the woman has no history of association with criminal types. She would have had to start from scratch, get just the right guy, and be able to totally trust him. That wouldn't happen in a matter of days. Two, the guy would have had to be aware of Brady's movements so he could follow him and strike at the perfect time. Brady had been out of town. No way for a hitman to know that. Three, the guy would have had to be a hell of an actor as well. He'd have had to make it look like it was a heist… make it seem like he panicked… make it appear he was so damn scared that he lost his own gun on the way out the door. Plus, he'd have to count on Brady doing something dumb during the robbery to make it look like it was spur-of-the-moment and not a hit."

"Does seem pretty far-fetched, doesn't it?"

"It does."

"Okay, I agree," Brig said. "But is it okay with you?"

"What do you mean? Is what okay with me?"

"I mean, is it okay for you to be ninety-nine-point-nine percent sure Brady killed Dane and be done with it? The Ed

Norman I used to know would have chewed off a leg and used it to hammer that last point-one percent nail into the coffin before calling it a day."

"You think we're the people we used to be, Brig? Are you? Sure, you still look the same. But do you still make the same decisions… the same way you did before? What about everything that's happened between the old days and now? What about time and circumstance?"

"I think it was you, Ed, who told me that people don't really change."

"Well, they mellow, that's for sure. At least I have. I've come to grips now with doing things that make the most sense, not the most noise. And I'm more than ready to let the D. A. know the Abel Dane case is closed, Dane's killer is dead, and justice has been damn well served… even if this Jocelyn Hayward gets to skate on a criminal conspiracy rap. Hell Brig, we've all got things in our past we've been lucky to get a pass on, right?"

"I damn sure have."

"So let's call it game, set, match. I'll tell the D. A. we're closing the cold case file. I'll let Jocelyn Hayward know we're wrapping things up without her involvement. And I'll have my boys know the only thing left to look into is the clumsy bandit who popped Brady. Are we good?"

"If you're good, my friend, I'm good."

But regardless of his reply, Ellis wasn't good. Not by a long shot.

CHAPTER 30

THE NIGHT HAD BECOME COOLER. After retrieving his car from the valet at Dan Tana's, Ellis got in, put the top down, and decided to drive a bit and clear his head before going back to the hotel. He turned right and went up the hill to Sunset Boulevard. As he cruised the famous thoroughfare, he was cognizant of the massive outdoor billboards, endless neon signs, and the pedestrian tide ebbing and flowing along the sidewalks. He saw it all, but he gave none of it any real thought. His mind had punched rewind, and he wasn't happy with what was replaying.

Let's add this up, Brig said to himself, as he started to reel off a string of disturbing facts, events, and occurrences. *One... Russo found it odd that Ed hadn't mentioned my involvement to him and Jamison until it was unavoidable. Two... I discovered Brady was out of town and I told Ed when the guy was returning. Three... even though Russo told me otherwise, I purposely asked Ed tonight about sending his detectives to the Brady homicide. He didn't correct me. Which means he may not have wanted me to know that he wasn't at the station when the killing went down. Four... when Ed pushed away from the table and crossed his leg tonight, I noticed he wasn't wearing his ankle gun. Five... Russo said*

Brady was shot with a .32 caliber Beretta. Same make, same caliber as the one Ed told me about when we had coffee the first day I was here. Six... when Ed laid out the case for why Jocelyn couldn't have found the right hitman, he actually made a case for why he would have been perfect for the job. Knowledge. Opportunity. Experience in covert ops... making one thing look like another... even going so far as to drop a gun that he knew couldn't be traced, to make it seem even more likely the perp was an amateur. Seven... lucky seven, or maybe unlucky *seven... Ed told me he'd let Jocelyn know she was off the hook, yet I was the one who'd met with her twice. I was the one she'd opened up to. Why does he want to be the one to get to her?*

Ellis now had a really bad feeling in the pit of his stomach. The *whats* fit into place, but the *whys* didn't. Why would Ed want Brady dead? The writer was already pegged to go down for the Dane killing. Why would Ed want to get with Jocelyn? Were they somehow in on something together? Or was she the last stone left unturned... the last living connection to the Abel Dane killing that might implicate Ed in some way?

Praying he wasn't too late, Ellis shifted out of cruising gear and floored it.

CHAPTER 31

AT JOCELYN HAYWARD'S SECURITY GATE, Ellis pushed the button and kept pushing until someone answered.

"Please stop that. Who is this?"

Recognizing the voice, Ellis said, "Jocelyn, it's me Brig Ellis. Are you alone?"

"It's late and I don't have anything to say to you."

"Jocelyn, just tell me if you're alone. Is anyone with you?"

The urgency in his voice prompted her to respond. "No. There's no one else here. But what does that matter? I still don't want to speak to you."

"Listen, Jocelyn, I need to talk to you. It's very important. You might be in danger."

"Danger. Danger from what… from whom? You said Brady might be dangerous, but he's dead."

"Look, some things have been happening. I need to talk to you about them. We can't have this conversation over the damn squawk box."

"Can't it wait until tomorrow? I was about to get in bed."

"No. It can't wait. We need to talk now. Buzz me in, please. It's important."

"Oh, all right. But this better be good."

Ellis heard the electronic sound, followed by the mechanical click of the gate unlocking. As soon as it had swung back far enough, he gunned his engine and raced inside. His haste was such that it didn't occur to him to watch the gate slowly close. Had he done so, he would have seen a man exit his parked car across the street and make it into the compound before the gate could shut him out.

Jocelyn met Ellis at her front door in a red and white kimono that was a floral mixture of satin, silk, and sensuality. Her hair was down and her face was free of makeup, but she still struck Ellis as one of the most beautiful women he had ever seen.

"May I come in?"

"Is this really necessary?"

"Please. We should talk."

"All right," she said as she stepped aside, let him in, and closed the door. Jocelyn then led the way to a great room that was surrounded on three of its four sides by floor-to-ceiling glass. She flopped onto one end of a white leather sofa and motioned for Ellis to take the far end. He did, involuntarily making a mental note that even her bare feet looked great.

"You've heard what happened to Brady?"

"It's been all over the news. I couldn't have missed it."

"I assume this has an impact on what you and I discussed the other day about taking your story to the District Attorney."

"I'm afraid I don't recall that particular conversation."

"I'm referring to the one we had at the Century Plaza Hotel."

"Yes. That's the one I don't remember. I can't recall it at all. And I assume you can easily see why it's not in my interest to do so."

"I can see how you might think that... based on media reports of a robbery gone bad, an impulse killing, a man simply in the wrong place at the wrong time."

"Then why are you here? And what is it that's so important?"

"I'm not convinced that Brady's death was a random act of violence."

"What do you mean?"

"I think it may have been orchestrated. You know, a setup."

"But who would do such a thing? And why?"

"The 'who' we'll come to. The 'why' is really the mysterious part."

"Please. No games. Just come to the point. Why would someone want Sam Brady dead?"

"Perhaps someone saw Brady as the last link in the conspiracy chain. The last person who could tie you to the Abel Dane murder. Is that pointed enough for you?"

Jocelyn looked honestly stunned. "Are you implying that I killed Brady? The news reports said some man did it. Are you seriously suggesting that I dressed up like a thug and convinced people in that bodega that I was some street criminal? You must think me quite the actress."

"No. I don't think you actually did it. But I am entertaining the idea that you might have had it done."

Shock quickly turned to anger in the timber of her voice. "That's crazy. I would never do something like that. Never. I wouldn't even know where to start. And if I did, why—"

Ellis cut her off. "Why kill someone to get out from under their control, only to seed control to whomever you hired?"

"Exactly," Jocelyn blurted. "Out of the frying pan and into the fire. I wouldn't do that."

"I don't think you would either," Ellis responded. "That's why I think you're in danger—danger from someone who wants to wipe the lottery slate clean."

"But who would that be... and why?"

The answer came not from Ellis, but from the other man

who had quietly entered through the front door and joined them in the great room. The man holding a gun on both of them as he said, "That would be me, Ms. Hayward."

Ellis and Jocelyn looked up to see Ed Norman standing before them. He had his service weapon, a Glock 9mm, pointed their way.

"After letting Mr. Ellis in, you neglected to lock the door. And Brig, you didn't watch your back after driving through the gate. It's the little things that sometimes lead to the most trouble, you know."

"I'll be mindful of that next time," Ellis replied. "Assuming there's going to be one."

"I wouldn't count on that, Brig. Circumstances simply may not allow it."

Jocelyn kept looking back and forth between each man. She wasn't exactly sure of what was going on, but she knew whatever it was, it didn't bode well.

Norman asked Ellis, "When did you put it together?"

"A bit earlier. When we were having dinner, I asked you about sending Russo and Jamison to the Bodega. You lied. Russo had already told me you were late getting in and they took the call from Santa Monica. It was a test. You didn't pass. I also noticed you weren't wearing your ankle gun at the restaurant. The one that just happens to be the same make and caliber as the one that killed Brady. Like you said, little things can make a big difference."

Norman let a tired smile cross his lips. "I guess we're both slipping, aren't we Brig?"

"We're a long way from where we were, that's for sure, Ed. I can't believe you're holding a gun on us."

Norman noticed a chair between where he stood and the two of them seated on the couch. He walked to the chair and sat down. Then he said, "Things don't always end the way we want them to."

Ellis wanted to keep his friend talking. He felt as long as they were conversing, there was a chance. "How did you want this one to end?"

"I hoped to wrap up what I had to do," Norman began, "and you'd go back to San Diego none the wiser."

"What was it you had to do, Ed? Why did you personally have to do anything? On that score, I don't have a clue. I found a motive for everyone else's involvement in Dane's death, but why would you take out Brady? And why the hell are you here now?"

"You said it earlier tonight, Brig. I'm the guy who can't rest until every 'i' is dotted and every 't' crossed. When me and mine are done wrong, I even the score. No matter how long it takes."

"You also indicated that you weren't that guy anymore."

"I lied. I had a sense you might be getting too close."

"But it's the *why* I still don't have. Why insert yourself in this? What does it all have to do with you?"

"I don't mind telling you now. Guess I owe you that much."

Ellis sat back to listen. This was something he definitely wanted to hear. Jocelyn pulled her feet up under her and dropped her hands into the pockets of her kimono. She had suddenly gotten a chill. Not from cold, from fear.

"The truth, Brig, and nothing but the truth? Okay. Why not? Kind of a sad story, really. It involves a lot of people that are dead… who didn't actually have to die. One thing sort of led to another and the dominoes started to fall. Let's start with Louise. You remember Louise, don't you, Brig? My wife. I told you about her. Definitely my better half. But I didn't tell you all about her. I didn't tell you how she got sick. Very sick. Doctors said she had pleural mesothelioma. Chalked it up to asbestos exposure at a factory she worked at long before we met. It's supposedly the deadliest cancer there is. The toughest to beat. When it started to metastasize, the medical experts here in the states said they had done everything they could for her. But we weren't ready to give up. We heard about this doctor in Mexico who had been reversing the growth of tumors with some pretty weird techniques—coffee enemas, daily injections of fluids with live cells from cattle and sheep, plus lots of laetrile. The treatment prospect sounded awful, but doing nothing sounded worse. Louise was a fighter. She was ready to give it a shot. The only problem was money. It was going to cost around a hundred thousand dollars for a one-month treatment. No U. S. insurance company was going to pay for that. And where was I going to get that kind of dough?

"Then it happened. There was this banquet. It was held by the city and various industries around Los Angeles to thank the police for helping them with public security when it's called for. My chief made me go. He said he couldn't make it. I wound up at this table with a bunch of movie types. One of them was Abel Dane. We got to talking about what he did and what I did. He wound up telling me the one thing he really wanted to do was a perfect crime story. Not just any crime. But a perfect murder story. You know, the kind where you really can't figure out who the killer actually is. Well, I couldn't get that thought out of my head. I kept knocking it around but I always came back to something I had seen or heard before. This one had to be different. This one had to be unsolvable. Then I hit upon it. Why not a lottery? A lottery where no one knows who draws the killing number except the killer. I got back to Dane. Told him I had a good idea. Went and talked to him about it. Asked him how much it might be worth. He said a story like that could garner a huge payday if it was served up to one of the studios by a big-time director. A director like him. He said he'd get his lawyer to work out a contract between us. An agreement spelling out that I gave him the idea for the original story, and that if it sold, I'd be paid the money I needed for Louise's treatment.

"I waited to hear back from him. First, it was days with one excuse after another. Each time he insisted on privacy so the story wouldn't be stolen. Then it was weeks and he began to duck my calls altogether. Then, before we knew it, Louise had tumors in different parts of her body. Doctors were afraid to operate because they thought her heart wasn't strong enough to take it. Neither of us was content to just let her waste away. They operated. She died on the table."

Ellis and Jocelyn had sat stone-faced through Norman's monologue. They weren't sure what to say, or when he'd stop.

"I was still at rock bottom some weeks later when Abel Dane was killed. Even though we didn't know who did it, I wanted to believe some kind of karma was involved. The bastard Dane got his because he robbed Louise of her last shot at life. But it kept eating at me for months and months. There had to be more to it than that. Eventually, I couldn't let it go. That's when I decided to bring you in, Brig, and when you found that stuff in Dane's desk, it all began to fall into place. The more we talked about it, the more we kicked it around, the more it became clear to me. Dane gave the lottery idea to Brady. He wanted Brady to use it in a script he could take to the studio. But Brady had an idea of his own. It wouldn't be a script. It would be a plan for the murder of Abel Dane. A perfect plan… where only the killer would know the killer's identity. So, you see, it wasn't just Dane that was responsible for Louise's death, and it wasn't just the person who pulled the trigger. It was everyone involved. Everyone who agreed to draw a number."

Brig interjected. "But how did Brady recruit the others? How'd he get them to go along?

"Perhaps we should ask one of the participants. How about it, Ms. Hayward?"

Jocelyn didn't know whether to answer or not. But she had already told Ellis of her involvement, and she feared that lying to the man with the gun in his hand would only anger him more. So she said, "Brady set his sights on people who seemed to be tethered to Dane whether they liked it or not. He got to know me and I told him as little as I could, but he could tell I despised Dane and that he had some kind of hold over me. I assume he did the same with the others. For whatever reason, we agreed to participate. The others probably hoped as I did… that with a one in five chance… they wouldn't have to be the one to do it. When I didn't draw number one, I thought I was lucky. I guess I was wrong."

"Luck comes and goes, Ms. Hayward. You had it for a while. Now you don't. That's just the way things are," Norman said. "What doesn't come and go… is retribution. Right, Brig? I mean we've brought down our share of God's vengeance on the wicked, have we not?"

Brig paused, then asked, "You're not putting yourself in God's place on this one, are you, Ed? That's a bit of a cop-out. You know what happened. You know who's responsible… both Dane and Brady. They're both dead. Brady by your own hand. Anything after that is on you. You have to own it."

"You think I can't? You'd be surprised at what I can own. What I can live with."

"Ed, you're not thinking clearly," Brig began. "All the others are dead. She already told you she didn't draw the killing number. And she's got no incentive to talk. It would just implicate her in a conspiracy. And what about me? What have I done to warrant this?"

"Look, Brig. I didn't plan it this way. Just counted on you getting me the info I needed, then you'd be gone. You dug a bit deeper than you should have. Now it needs to be cleaned up."

"Cleaned up? Is that what you call this? After all we've been through together."

"We did have our moments, didn't we, Brig?"

"Seems to me, I might have saved your life as often as you saved mine."

"That's probably true, mate. I tell you what. You're right. History is important. Particularly our history. It was pretty damned meaningful. So maybe the least I can do is give you a shot. You know, one last chance to see which of us still has what it takes."

"What are you talking about?"

"We certainly won't go hand-to-hand. You're in a lot better shape than me. I know you're packing. So in a moment, I'll lay my gun on this end table beside me. See that clock over the mantle? When the second hand on that clock hits 12, we'll both go for our guns. Like the Wild West, you know. You won't go early because that's the kind of guy you are. I won't go early because I need to see if I'm anywhere near the man I used to be. If I take you out, I make up some story that during the course of your investigation you became obsessed with Ms. Hayward. Obsession's always a believable story in Hollywood. I simply say I didn't arrive in time to stop you from killing her, but I was able to get you before you got me."

Jocelyn turned to Ellis and said. "Please. No. You don't owe me your life. I'm the one who got myself into this."

Ellis responded. "If Ed wasn't the kind of guy he is, I wouldn't be getting any chance at all." Then he turned slightly on the couch and planted both feet firmly on the floor, saying to himself, *Maybe I can jump him just before the second-hand hits twelve. Then none of us will wind up dead.*

"Thirty seconds from launch, Brig. I'm going to lay my piece down now. Keep your eyes on that clock. We both go when the hand hits twelve."

Ellis felt the seconds ticking away faster than they ever had before. The muscles in his legs tightened. His hand dropped to his side to make it look more like he was preparing to reach for his gun rather than getting ready to propel himself from the couch.

Fifteen seconds to go. Then ten. Nine. Eight. Seven...

Gunshots roared with terrifying ferocity as one, then another bullet rocketed from the silk pocket of Jocelyn's kimono, the explosions causing her garment to catch fire.

Stunned for just a moment, Ellis jumped up and began beating the flame out as he simultaneously stared at Norman. The detective's eyes were wide with shock as his white shirt turned crimson.

"I had to shoot," Jocelyn cried. "He was going to kill us."

Ellis left her quivering on the couch and went over to Norman. As he bent down, he saw that the slugs had passed through both man and chair and landed in the wall behind him. The holes in the front of the policeman's torso were small but the exit wounds were starting to soak the chair with dark blood.

Norman's eyes were open but they seemed to be staring beyond Ellis.

"Should've made... turn pockets out... right, Brig?"

Before Ellis could answer, blood came up Norman's throat and slid out the side of his mouth.

"Damn it," was all Ellis could think to say.

CHAPTER 32

THE APPROPRIATE CALL WAS MADE. Ellis instructed Jocelyn not to touch anything until the authorities arrived. The great room was a crime scene now and it was not to be disturbed. He even kept her from changing clothes or washing her hands until the police arrived. When they did, Russo and Jamison were with them. Russo pulled Ellis aside and asked Jamison to get a statement from Jocelyn. The P. I. just stood there, looking at his former boss still sitting in a chair with two bullet holes in his chest.

"Want to tell me what happened," Russo asked.

Ellis took the detective through the events that had transpired, including his dinner with Norman that preceded his coming to Jocelyn's home. He went on to repeat Norman's confession about his wife's illness, and his intent to eliminate anyone that had anything to do with keeping them from getting the money they needed for her experimental treatments. Russo listened intently, made a note or two along the way, but didn't respond with as much surprise as Ellis thought he might.

"So basically," Russo began, "you're saying that Ed killed Brady and faked it as a botched robbery. Then he came here to take out Ms. Hayward, but you got in first. So he was going to have to kill both of you?"

"She obviously believed that. And she couldn't take a chance on me getting the best of him. That's why she fired."

Pointing to Norman's weapon still on the end table, Russo asked, "That the piece he was holding on you guys?"

"Yes," Brig replied.

Russo walked over, took the pen he had been making notes with and slipped it in the barrel to pick it up. He was about to give it to the CSI investigator for bagging when a strange look crossed his face. He held it up and jiggled it a bit. "Kind of light," he said. Then he set it back down, and being as careful as he could not to mix his own prints with those already on the gun, he ejected the magazine, which was empty.

Russo said, "So, a seasoned police officer challenged his old mate to a gun fight, and was maybe going to kill a possible suspect in the Dane killing with an unloaded Glock. Something here's not kosher."

Ellis paused before responding. Then said, "You worked with Ed for a long time. Did he seem different lately?"

"Depends on what you mean by 'lately'. Fact is, Ed became a different guy after his wife died. Kept to himself. Seemed to have more run-ins with the brass at work. Even on good days, never seemed to crack a joke anymore, or even enjoy one. When he did this thing with you, well, we were all a bit put off, you know?"

"What do you mean 'this thing' with me?"

"Bringing you in on the Dane cold case. Keeping you isolated from the guys who worked it initially. Only getting Jamison and me involved when it started to get out of hand. And fronting the whole thing himself."

"Fronting? What are you talking about?"

"What do you think? He was paying for you out of his own

pocket? You don't believe the LAPD would actually put you up in some fancy-schmancy hotel, pick up per diem tabs, and pay you a fee to boot, do you? Look, I handle all the paperwork for our division. There was no funding request for outside consultation on the Dane cold case. Ed brought you in on his own dime."

"I had no idea."

"And I guess he thought it was time to wrap up the whole shebang," Russo said.

"Meaning?"

"Well, look at it this way. He offs Brady. Tells you what he thinks you want to hear so you'll run to the rescue of the Hayward broad. Then he braces you both with an unloaded gun. He was bringing the curtain down. He'd had enough of the case, enough of life, enough of everything. He was planning on you gunning him because he gave you no other choice. Sort of a reverse form of death by cop. From his point of view, the case was solved, the guilty punished. I guess he saw no reason to keep going. The shrinks say if grief and depression are strong enough, some people just decide there's no point in going on."

Ellis heard everything Russo said and while he hated to admit it about his old friend, it seemed to make sense. But there was still Jocelyn Hayward.

"So," Ellis asked Russo, "you going to charge her with anything?"

"If her statement to Jamison lines up with yours, I don't see any point. Cut and dried case of self-defense. Even though she shot first, she thought she was about to be killed. Jury would never convict, and for that matter, the D. A. would probably never take it to court in the first place."

"What about her admission of this conspiracy to kill Dane?"

"Got anything other than her confession to you?"

"No. Though I did tell Ed."

"Ed obviously won't be confirming that. Think she'll cop to it now that no one's around to corroborate?"

"No. I don't."

"I don't either." Russo then added, "and frankly, the department's going to want to keep all of this as quiet as possible. When a member of the team's involved, it's bad form to gin up a lot of publicity. Officially, the Brady killing will likely stay unsolved and get listed as a stick-up gone bad. It's a good bet you won't be reading much in the days ahead about this incident either. Hayward's a studio asset, they won't want to throw a monkey wrench into that. And she'll be happy to put a lid on it. Not good for her career. Plus she won't want to circle back regarding involvement in Dane's death. The department will likely be more than happy to sweep the whole thing under the rug. Officer killed in the line of duty. Accidental. Case of mistaken identity. The lady thought he was a burglar. That sort of thing. Only speed bump standing in the way of putting it all to bed is you. And I can't see that anything that you might add would help Ed or his reputation in any way. Can you?"

"Think that's what Ed cared about, his reputation? I don't. I think, in addition to his wife, he cared about what he always cared about... settling the score."

CHAPTER 33

A DAY AFTER WHAT HE HAD come to think of as one of the worst nights of his life, Ellis checked out of The Chateau Marmont and drove to Robertson Boulevard in Beverly Hills where Jocelyn had agreed to meet him for a farewell lunch at The Ivy. It was one of those classic eateries where film folk and business types gather to see and be seen. Cloistered among shade trees, the old brick building that housed the restaurant was covered in the green wonder that bore its name. Both indoor and outdoor tables were festooned with red, yellow, and orange roses that were almost as pretty as the drinks and desserts that were served there.

Jocelyn had arrived before Ellis and was seated at a relatively secluded table beneath one of the spreading eucalypti trees. She raised her napkin as he walked onto the patio but it was really unnecessary. Although she was still somewhat masked by her oversized sunglasses, her raven hair, perfect nose, and full mouth would have caught his eye anywhere. He joined her, saw that she was having a mojito, and told the waiter he'd have one as well.

"Have you recovered somewhat from last night?" He asked.

"Somewhat would be the operative word. How about you?"

"I guess I'm as good as I can be," Ellis began.

"I am so sorry for what happened. I was just so frightened."

"No one's blaming you. I'm certainly not. Ed put us in an untenable situation. There was no good way out of it. I just hate that his life and his state of mind turned on him like it did."

"Yes, the other policeman told me about the discussion you two had. I guess your friend was just another poor soul you can add to those done wrong by Abel Dane."

The waiter returned with Ellis's drink and Jocelyn told him they would order in a little while.

"I'm glad you asked to see me before you returned to San Diego," Jocelyn said. "I was hoping we wouldn't have to part as… you know… enemies… or anything like that."

"Why would we be enemies?"

"Well, the fact that I didn't want to tell anyone else about what I told you that day at the Century Plaza. It just seemed that there was no longer any reason to do so. I couldn't see any good that could come of it. Not for me, or my son."

"I can understand that," Ellis replied. "People have to look out for themselves in this world. Especially if they're responsible for someone else too."

"I'm so looking forward to having him with me. Can't remember if I mentioned it to you, but I'm seeing an attorney soon to begin the legal proceedings to make it happen."

"You're quite the woman. A lot of people in your position, with a thriving career and all, wouldn't want to take on a child at this point in their lives."

"Some wouldn't. But I can't wait. This life isn't really as glamorous as it's made out to be. It can get lonely. Plus, I have my family to help me. We're still very close. That's why the thought of terminating my pregnancy never entered the picture. I always hoped one way or another that my son and

I would be able to be together someday."

"Even though his father was such a… what's the euphemism for it… a cad?"

"Yes. Abel was awful. But maybe our son is the one good thing that will have come from his contemptible life."

"Well, you obviously love the child. You've got the financial resources to give him a good start in life. Plus a supporting family to help along the way. I think you're both going to be more than okay."

"Thank you for saying that. And thank you for all you've done. Without your involvement, who knows how all of this might have ended?"

Ellis let the compliment slide, and simply said, "So, are you hungry?"

"I am. Let's order."

Over lunch, their conversation turned more cordial. She asked him about the kinds of situations a private investigator normally gets involved in. He quizzed her about upcoming films she might be starting. They both commiserated over the losses of Iris Stanton, Zack Richards, Yuri Kaminski, Sam Brady, and Ed Norman. Neither voiced any particular concern over the passing of Abel Dane. Over coffee, however, Ellis felt that the trust factor was strong enough and the mood was such that he could bring up something that had been on his mind for quite a while.

"You know one of the things that always bugged me about the Dane case, is how the gun that killed him was never found. I mean, from the moment the police arrived, I assumed they searched the personal effects of every person they interviewed, every suspect's room, perhaps even every room in the hotel. But the gun was never found. How could that be? Was getting rid of the gun part of the original plan?"

Jocelyn hesitated for a moment, but she too now felt a bond between her and Ellis. She began, "Brady's plan…"

"You mean Norman's plan," Ellis interjected.

"Oh yes, that's right. Well, put it this way: Brady's execution of Norman's plan called for whoever had to eliminate Abel to dispose of the gun, too. And he explained to everyone long before numbers were ever drawn how that could be done. Have you ever noticed how many hotel rooms have counter space for coffee, and incidentals and things like that? Sometimes you just drop your bags or whatever on those counters or under them. Well, the point is, nobody ever looks at the underside of the counter. I mean even when the maids come in to clean up, they just run the vacuum cleaners under them to sweep the carpet, or they wipe the tops when they clean them off. But they never look under them. There's no need. So the plan was that whoever drew Number One and did the deed, well, that person would then tape the gun to the underside of the counter—using gaffer's tape that's on every film set. That stuff will hold anything in place. Then, after an appropriate amount of time had passed, that person would make another reservation at the hotel on the condition that they have the same room they had before. When they returned, they'd take the gun away and dispose of it. Abel would be gone. The gun would be gone. And still, the individuals who didn't draw Number One would never know who did."

"Pretty slick," Ellis commented. "So tell me, do you have any idea who actually killed Abel Dane?"

Jocelyn took off her sunglasses, looked Ellis directly in the eyes, and said, "No. I really don't. I only know it wasn't me. And I'm so sorry for being part of something that led to so much sadness and death."

"We all get involved in things we shouldn't," Ellis replied. "Things we can't go back and change. All we can do is try not to repeat our mistakes."

Each looked at the other without saying anything for a moment. When the pregnant pause became uncomfortable, Ellis broke the silence.

"Well, listen... if you ever have occasion to come down to San Diego, I hope you'll give me a call. You know we have an absolutely world-class zoo. Any youngster would have a great time there."

"I'd like that. I really would. And I'm sure my son would too. Do you think there's any chance you might be coming back to Los Angeles in the future?"

"There's always a chance. Especially if there's an invitation."

"When things get sorted out, I wouldn't be at all surprised if you got one."

Ellis reached into his pocket, pulled out his business card and handed it to her. She read it out loud.

"*Investigations, Security, Confidential Matters.* That covers a lot of ground. Which do you think we might be involved in one day?"

"The latter, I would hope. But call anytime... even if it's just to talk. I'd like to know how things work out with you and the boy."

Jocelyn reached over and grasped his hand, "You're a good man, Brig Ellis. Even with all that's happened, I've very glad we came into each other's life."

He stared at her for an instant and realized he was on the verge of saying something that would likely make him sound like a dope. So, he simply replied, "Me, too."

CHAPTER 34

AFTER LEAVING THE RESTAURANT, ELLIS had already decided to take the coast road back to San Diego. It was a sunny day, not too hot, and with the top down, the breeze and smell of the ocean were just what he needed to try to clear his head of the past week's events. They'd never be completely gone, he knew. The time he'd shared with Iris Stanton, meeting Jocelyn Hayward, reconnecting with Ed Norman then losing him the way he did—these were things that would remain in his internal hard drive long after weeks, months, maybe even years had passed. He'd do his best, however, to simply chalk up what had happened to the crazy dichotomy of life and death, in all its infinite variety. But then something swung back into his thoughts, lodged, and stayed there. Eventually, it forced him to pull off the highway onto the shoulder of the road. With the beach and the surf on his right, the waves spilling on shore then retreating like a lover's playful game of tag, his mind ran back to his conversation with Jocelyn. She had given him the end game. She had told him what he needed to know. She had provided the key to solving the mystery of who killed Abel Dane. He could simply take out his cell phone, call Detective Russo, tell him to have the Chateau Marmont check their records to see which of the five suspects had later booked an overnight stay in the same room they had occupied previously. Whoever did that was the killer. It was that simple.

But, Ellis thought to himself. Should I call? What good will it do? Yes, he'll know who killed the man that was responsible for so much pain and anguish. But is unmasking Dane's killer really that important now? Jocelyn indicated that she was willing to never know. The police believed it might be best to bury the whole thing until no one is interested anymore. But what about Ed? Ed, who was going to carry through no matter the price. What about Ed?

The phone at the police station rang and was quickly answered.

"Russo here."

"Detective, this is Brig Ellis."

"Hey, Ellis. I was wondering if you'd call before you took off."

"I was planning to… then I wasn't… then I changed my mind."

"Well, I appreciate you calling. I hope you have a safe trip, man."

"Russo, there is one thing… one piece of information… that only came to light a little while ago. I think it would be valuable for you to know about it."

"Lay it on me."

"Whoever killed Abel Dane… wound up hiding the murder weapon in their room."

"I understand that all the rooms were searched. Nothing was found."

"Regardless… you need to check with The Chateau Marmont and see which of the five suspects booked a room there some time after the killings. Specifically, which of them booked a stay with the proviso that they had to have the same room they were in the night of the killing."

"You're trying to tell me that the killer hid the gun somewhere it couldn't be found in his or her room… just let it stay there… and then came back later to retrieve and dispose of it?"

"That's what I'm saying, Detective Russo."

"Sounds a bit like that old cliché of the killer returning to the scene of the crime."

"There's a reason clichés exist. There's always a grain of truth in all of them."

"How'd you come by this information?"

"Does it really matter?"

"Nah, I guess not. But you realize, Ellis, even if we found that one of the individuals came back and stayed in the same room they stayed in before, we won't have any proof that they retrieved a gun and then got rid of it. We still won't be able to prove anything."

"It's not about proof."

"No. Then what the hell's it about?"

"Closure."

Russo paused before answering "Yeah. I see what you mean. I'll look into it. Want me to let you know what I find out?"

"I'm not at all sure I do… but let me know anyway."

Ellis turned off his phone, took a last, long look at the sea, then swung back onto the coast highway. He was heading home, more than ready to put Hollywood in his rearview mirror.

EPILOGUE

A DAY AFTER RETURNING FROM LOS Angeles, Ellis was walking his English bulldog, Osgood, through San Diego's Balboa Park. The dog, like Ellis, enjoyed being outdoors and his rumbling gait—somewhat like a Christmas ham constantly rolling left and right—put a smile on the faces of people they passed. The duo had stopped at Prado and were sitting at one of the outside tables sharing an ABC (avocado, bacon, and cheese) Burger when Ellis's cell phone emitted its signature ring, the opening notes of Warren Zevon's *Werewolves of London*. Ellis noted the L.A. area code but he wasn't sure whose number it was. Still, he thought it best to answer before the other patrons of the restaurant became too annoyed at his ringtone.

"This is Brig Ellis."

"Hey, Ellis. Russo here. Catch you at a good time?"

"Sure. My dog and I are just enjoying another one of these beautiful San Diego days. Sitting in the sun, enjoying the scenery, filling our bellies with things that we shouldn't."

"Well, I envy you. We've got another smog alert day."

"Why am I not surprised?"

"When we talked yesterday," Russo began, "you said you learned that the killer had hidden the weapon in the room so well that we never found it. And that the person probably came back later, made sure they got the same room, then took it away with them when they left."

"That's what I said."

"Well, we checked with the hotel, but they couldn't find any record of one of our five suspects re-booking with them in the days, weeks, or even months after the shooting."

"You don't say," Ellis responded. "Hard for me to believe I was misled."

"Well, we all get hoodwinked from time to time. Such is our lot in life, I suppose."

Ellis, still unwilling to let it go completely, gave it one last shot. "Did the hotel personnel tell you anything at all about *anyone* insisting they be given the same room as they had before?"

"The hotel manager mentioned that some celebrities and their agents do that from time to time. But it's usually for the bigger suites only. Though they did tell us about one request they got for a certain room in the hotel. Said they had no record that the person had ever stayed with them before. But they stressed that the individual on the phone who was making the reservation was absolutely adamant. Refused to accept anything other than one particular room."

"Did they give you that person's name?"

"They did. It's here somewhere. Just a second. Oh, yeah. Here it is. A Ms. Maria Flores."

"Say that again."

"Maria Flores. Ring a bell?"

"Russo, how well did you examine each of the background files on the suspects?"

"Well, you know, as well as we usually do... as well as time permits."

"Two of the suspects were actors, weren't they?"

"That's right. Two of them."

"And both of us, being old movie fans, know that sometimes actors adopt stage names, don't they?"

"They do indeed. In fact, as I recall, Cary Grant was a stage name. His real name was Archie Leach. And Tony Curtis's real name was actually Bernie Schwartz. Can you believe that?"

"And if you take a little closer look at one of the background files," Ellis said, "you'll see that Maria Flores is the real name of Jocelyn Hayward."

"No shit?"

"No shit."

Russo bellowed, "But she swore up and down that she didn't do it."

"That's what she swore."

"That means she killed both Dane and Ed."

"That's what it means."

"And we can't get her on either one, can we? Damn. She gets a pass for Ed because it was self-defense. And she skates on the Dane murder because while we might be able to place her coming back to the hotel under her real name, we can't prove she recovered the murder weapon and disposed of it. We don't have proof of anything."

"Actually, we do have proof of one thing."

"Oh yeah. What's that?"

"We have proof she's one hell of an actress."

After finishing their lunch, Ellis and Osgood took one more turn through the park to aid their digestion. Osgood wondered how many squirrels he might run across, and where the best grassy knolls might rise, to relieve himself if necessary. Ellis wondered how long it would take him to get over everything that went down in L.A., and whether he would ever hear from Jocelyn Hayward again… and what he might do if he did.

Then he looked at the mound of mutt sauntering at the end of his leash and said, "Osgood, did you know there once was a time when sad stories had happy endings?"

The bulldog declined to reply.

ABOUT THE AUTHOR

JOE KILGORE has won awards for novels, novellas, screenplays, and short stories. His tales have appeared in magazines, creative journals, anthologies, and online literary publications. He is the author of *Insomniac: Short Stories for Long Nights. Cast Them Dead* is his third Brig Ellis Tale, after *Fool's Errand*, and *Dying Art. Carrion Moon*, the fourth in the series, is in the works. His other novels include *The Horse Killer*, *A Farmhouse in the Rain*, *The Blunder*, and *The Golden Dancer*.

Prior to writing fiction, he had a long and successful career creating, writing, and producing television and radio commercials, plus newspaper, magazine, and internet content for an international advertising agency. He also writes novel reviews professionally for national and international firms. He lives in Austin, Texas, with his wife, Claudia, an accomplished artist. You can read more about Joe and his writing at his website: https://joekilgore.com.

www.ingramcontent.com/pod-product-compliance
Lightning Source LLC
Chambersburg PA
CBHW050323110726
47899CB00007B/2354